Theodore G. Thomas, Frederick A. Porcher

A Contribution to the History of the Huguenots

of South Carolina, consisting of pamphlets

Theodore G. Thomas, Frederick A. Porcher

A Contribution to the History of the Huguenots
of South Carolina, consisting of pamphlets

ISBN/EAN: 9783337293598

Printed in Europe, USA, Canada, Australia, Japan

Cover: Foto ©Andreas Hilbeck / pixelio.de

More available books at **www.hansebooks.com**

A CONTRIBUTION

TO THE

HISTORY OF THE HUGUENOTS

OF SOUTH CAROLINA

CONSISTING OF PAMPHLETS

BY

SAMUEL DUBOSE, Esq.
OF ST. JOHN'S BERKELEY, SOUTH CAROLINA
AND
Prof. FREDERICK A. PORCHER
OF CHARLESTON, SOUTH CAROLINA

REPUBLISHED FOR PRIVATE CIRCULATION

BY

T. GAILLARD THOMAS, M.D.

NEW YORK
The Knickerbocker Press
1887

INTRODUCTION.

The accompanying historical sketches of the Huguenot families which settled in the rich alluvial regions within fifty miles of Charleston will prove of interest to but few.

While the modern historian seeks with eagerness all records which tell of the Knickerbocker and the Puritan, who left their impress clear, distinct, and strong upon the country of their adoption, little interest attaches to the Huguenot, who played a less important rôle in making history and in writing his name upon its pages.

To a certain number of the descendants of those devoted men, however, who, in consequence of the revocation of the Edict of Nantes by the harsh and impolitic act of Louis XIV., settled in various parts of this country, faithful sketches like these to which this serves as preface, will be prized as contributions towards that thus far unwritten " History of the Huguenot Emigrants to America," which I feel sure must erelong appear.

Actuated by these considerations, I have thought that a reproduction of the simple, modest, and faithful recitals of things which came under the personal observation of these writers, and which have long since been out of print, would give pleasure to some of the friends of my youth, preserve facts for future use which would otherwise be lost, and give to my own children an opportunity of learning something concerning their forefathers which is not recorded elsewhere.

I need hardly say that these pamphlets have been left exactly as they came from the hands of the writers, and that they have been reproduced only for private circulation.

THEODORE GAILLARD THOMAS, M.D.

NEW YORK

CONTENTS.

ADDRESS

DELIVERED AT THE SEVENTEENTH ANNIVERSARY OF THE

BLACK OAK AGRICULTURAL SOCIETY

ON TUESDAY, APRIL 27, 1858.

BY SAMUEL DUBOSE, ESQ.

PRESIDENT OF THE SOCIETY

TO WHICH IS ADDED, REMINISCENCES OF ST. STEPHEN'S PARISH AND NOTICES
OF HER OLD HOMESTEADS, BY SAMUEL DUBOSE, ESQ.

Published at the Request of the Black Oak Agricultural Society

ADDRESS.

Gentlemen of the Black Oak Agricultural Society :

At your last anniversary meeting, the following resolution was passed, to wit :

" *Resolved*, That the President be requested to prepare, for the next anniversary meeting of the Society, an historical account of the introduction of cotton-planting into this section of country ; together with short biographical sketches or reminiscences of the earlier planters who were instrumental in its cultivation—detailing the progress made in its culture and preparation for market, in the climatizing of the finer qualities of cotton, whether by selection of seed grown here or by importation from the sea islands, with a comparison of the productiveness of our lands at its earliest cultivation with the old Santee "black seed" and that of the present time with the finer island seed, and all other points of historical interest connected with the progress and development of our staple crop."

It will be readily admitted, gentlemen, that prudence ought to have deterred me from attempting a compliance with your wish thus expressed ; having no record or reference, but thrown altogether upon memory, stretching back over a period of more than sixty years. I have, however, been induced by the desire to comply with the requirements of a Society over which your partiality has called me to preside.

It is strange and true that human life is made up
of the past and future circumstances and events
that have been and are to come.   Behind us lies a
wide waste, strewed with the wrecks of blasted
hopes and wasted efforts.   In our onward progress
we grasp at a point of time which we call the present.   A moment intervenes, and that moment is
gone forever.   Often would we linger long and
fondly around those cherished scenes where earthly
joys shed their brightest rays—but in vain ; the current sweeps on, and those scenes lie behind us, and
joys which made them bright shall be felt no more.
Memory belongs to the past ; it lingers among the
joys that are fled ; it tells of what we have done in
the days that are gone ; it goes back to the record
of the past.   Memory belongs to the aged.   Hope
revels in the beauties of the morning of life, but its
promise is often delusive.   Through the journey of
life, it is always sweet to review the happy scenes
that we have witnessed in other days : the pleasing
associations of childhood, the friends we loved,
the joys we felt, the affections we indulged,—all
come up like a sweet dream from the depths of the
past, and breathe a fragrance upon the spirit in the
later years of life.   But to proceed :

In the year 1689 a colony of French Huguenots,
numbering about one hundred and eighty families,
arrived in Carolina, settled themselves on the Santee, in St. James' Parish, and called their town

James Town. Their purchase of lands was made from the numerous and warlike tribe of Indians called the Santees. With these people they lived in remarkable friendship, doing them no wrong or injustice. They cultivated the soil for their immediate necessities. As soon as compatible with circumstances, they commenced improving their pecuniary condition by the cultivation of the staple products of the soil and the manufacture of naval stores. These, as well as indigo dye and rice, were articles of prime necessity to the mother country. She stimulated their production by a bounty upon the articles sent to market. Naval stores were a profitable and healthy pursuit to those who were advantageously located, and Watboo afforded a convenient landing. Fortunes were made by those who engaged in the business with attention and judgment. Among the most successful was John Palmer, of Gravel Hill. He commenced life poor, and left at his death about one hundred negroes to each of his children. In the course of a few years many of the descendants of the colony, finding the river swamp lands higher up, in what afterward became St. Stephen's Parish, to be safer from freshets, gradually bought lands and moved up to the whole extent of the parish, until it became the most densely populated portion of the State out of Charleston. The entire swamp was in like manner populated with slaves. In some cases the owners and most of the overseers resided on the plantations through the year. Indigo was a light and beautiful crop ; the whole process of changing it from the weeds into the matured dry lumps was a very nice and critical one, requiring untiring attention during night and day ; a periodical change of hands was required throughout the time, with the exception of him called the indigo maker, who could no more leave his post of responsibility, than could the captain of a ship on a lee shore.

Rice also began to be cultivated as a crop ; at first on high land and on little spots of low ground, as they were met with here and there. These low grounds being found to agree better with the plant, the inland swamps were cleared for the purpose of extending the culture. In the course of time, as the fields became too grassy and stubborn, they were abandoned for new clearings, and so on ; until at length the superior adaptation of the tide-lands was discovered, and their great facilities for irrigation. The inland plantations were gradually abandoned for these, and that great body of land, which little more than a century ago furnished for exportation over 50,000 barrels of rice, now lies utterly waste. Just previous to the Revolution, the tax returns exhibited upwards of 5,000 slaves within the parish, or rather in Santee swamp, there being then no settlements out of its limits.

Few planters failed of acquiring an independence,

and many made fortunes large for the times and circumstances. Among the planters most successful at this business was Peter Sinkler, who, without any property with which to begin life, went daily with his hoe-cake and axe to his labor. At his death, about twenty-five years afterwards, he left for his children three valuable plantations and upwards of three hundred slaves. He died in Charleston a prisoner to the British, under the most cruel treatment. Before he was carried from his plantation he was made to witness the destruction of the following property, viz. : twenty thousand pounds of indigo worth one dollar and fifty cents a pound, one hundred and thirty head of cattle, one hundred and fifty-four head of sheep, two hundred head of hogs, three thousand bushels of grain, twenty thousand rails, household furniture valued at £2,500; besides carrying off fifty-five negroes, sixteen blood horses, and twenty-eight mares and colts.

Peter Sinkler was a man remarkable for wonderful endurance, industry, and skill in the pursuit of his business. His parent could afford him only six months' schooling, when the necessities of a widowed mother and sister required the labor of himself and brother at home. When the Revolution broke out he devoted himself to the service of his country. From strong traits of character he soon possessed much influence among his fellow-citizens. This the enemy became aware of, and determined to make an

example of him.   Like others of the Whigs, he was
wont occasionally to fly from the privations and
fatigues endured by the soldiers of Marion's brigade to recruit within the bosom of his family.
The enemy having ascertained this determined, if
possible, to capture him.   His own brother-in-law,
James Boisseau, who had enjoyed no other home
but his, was won over by bribery to betray him.
He was captured in the manner following.   His
house was situated within fifty yards of the Santee
swamp, and it was his habit, when necessary in
order to avoid the danger which threatened from
the front, to retire by the back way to his usual
place of concealment.   Boisseau, with a sufficient
force below, threaded his way to the spot at which
he knew Mr. Sinkler would enter it.   Soon after a
force was seen descending the avenue.   The victim
took his hat and returning to his place of concealment found himself in the arms of his captors.
He was refused an interview with his wife and
daughters, made to witness the destruction of the
property as specified, carried off a prisoner to the
provost in Charleston, and there, without a change
of clothes, he was thrust into the southeast room of
the post-office cellar, among a crowd as unfortunate
as himself, without bedding or even straw to lie
upon.   Typhus fever soon terminated their sufferings.   As his reward Boisseau enjoyed for life a
commission in the British army and a civil station
in Nova Scotia.

At the period of which we write men were much more laborious and devoted to their business than at the present day; a fact or two will prove this. During the period of manufacturing the indigo dye, which was a process requiring the closest attention, Mr. Sinkler though he slept every night in his bed, never for three weeks saw the face of his wife or daughters; he returned and departed while they slept. He and his brother lived full twelve miles asunder, and yet they generally visited each other after dark; they would eat supper and then return home. All this was done on horseback, sulkies and buggies being then unknown.

Upon the resort of the planters to the inland swamps for the cultivation of rice, the work of reclamation and preparation for rendering them safe and productive was both arduous and precarious; subject as they were as often to an excess of water, as to a want of it when most needed. It is now a source of surprise and wonder to examine the amount of labor and skill some of the fields in this neighborhood exhibit. Take, for instance, Wantoot, the patrimonial estate of Daniel Ravenel, Esq., who died in 1807. On his land four swamps unite to form Biggin, each contributing copious streams. To unite and concentrate these into one, and bear off the water when in excess, as well as distribute it into the fields of the different plantations, called for judgment, perseverance, and an amount of labor not easily understood.   Mr. Ravenel resided in Charleston during the summer months when the work had to be chiefly carried on, and from thence he issued his orders to his driver, who occasionally went to town to receive them.   On these occasions, for his better understanding of his master's wishes, the carpet would be taken from the floor of the hall, and a plat of the swamp, the creeks, watercourses, etc., chalked out for the driver's study and understanding. This man was slow of understanding, but very faithful and assiduous in executing his master's wishes. His success was a matter of wonder to the community around.

The war terminated this state of prosperity.   On the return of peace every planter was deeply in debt.   For the period of ten years following no income was realized on account of freshets ; in many cases not even provisions.   Prime gangs of negroes were publicly sold at an average of less than two hundred dollars.   Rice and indigo and naval stores became of little value, because of the loss of the bounty formerly allowed under the colonial system.

The British government, ever true to her colonial policy, raised up in rivalry the culture of the indigo, both in their West and East India possessions. Besides all this, they who held property in paper were either not paid or paid in worthless, depreciated money ; and to complete the threatened ruin of the planters, the frequency of the freshets in the swamps forced the owners to abandon the cultivation of these lands, but recently so valuable. To make this better understood, let the fact be stated that Milford plantation, containing one hundred acres of high land and four or five hundred of swamp, which had been sold for six thousand guineas, was abandoned at the time we are speaking of as almost worthless.

The people, however, inspired by the success of their struggles and sufferings for liberty, did not despond nor slacken their exertions ; they manufactured cloth for their families and slaves ; they raised every thing needful for consumption. The necessities of the war, and the state of things existing for some time after it, greatly increased the number of domestic fabrications of the wool, until about the year 1790, when the practice of using homespun for plantation purposes became very common throughout the parishes and districts. The yarn was spun at home and sent to the nearest weaver. Among the manufacturing establishments, the one near Murray's Ferry, in Williamsburg, owned by Irish settlers, supplied the adjacent country. The cotton for the spinning process was prepared in general by the field laborers, who, in addition to their ordinary work, picked the seed from the wool at the rate of four pounds of clean cotton per week.

In the year 1794 the Santee Canal was commenced. This gave employment to nearly all the

working negroes in the parish at high and remunerative wages.   This enterprise relieved the planters
of a burden which oppressed them, and left them
partially untrammelled to prepare for the new staple
which had been for some time exciting their hopes.

As far back as 1790 attempts had been made to
plant cotton as a market crop in different localities
of the Southern country.   Even at an earlier period,
among the exports from Charleston to Great Britain
in 1748, we find seven bags of cotton wool valued at
£3 11s. 6d. per bag.   In 1754 some cotton was
again exported from South Carolina.   In 1770
there were shipped to Liverpool three bags from
New York, four bags from Virginia and Maryland,
and three barrels from North Carolina.   In 1794 an
American vessel that carried eight bags to Liverpool
was seized, on the ground that so much cotton could
not be the product of the United States.

In 1785, fourteen bags ; in 1786, six bags ; in
1787, one hundred and nine bags ; in 1788, three
hundred and eighty-nine bags ; in 1789, eight hundred and forty-two bags ; in 1790, eighty-one
bags.   The bag of cotton first sold in South
Carolina was purchased in 1784 by John Teas-
dale, from Bryan Cape, then a factor in Charleston.   The export of cotton slowly but steadily
increased until 1794, when a powerful impetus was
given to the cotton culture by the invention of the
saw gin by Eli Whitney of Massachusetts.

In Georgia the long-staple cotton was first planted for market ; in Virginia, North Carolina, and South Carolina, the short-staple.

As early as 1787 small quantities of cotton in the seed were brought from Orangeburg district and sold to merchants at 2d. per pound, who resold it principally to ladies to make patch-work bedquilts.

When Whitney's saw gin was first exhibited in Georgia, none but women were permitted to enter the room. An ingenious young mechanic introduced himself into the apartment in women's apparel, and by a minute examination of the machine satisfied himself that he could not only imitate but improve on its construction by making it more efficient. The gins so constructed were first applied to water-power by General Wade Hampton.

The first attempt to raise a crop of long cotton in South Carolina was in 1788, by Kinsey Burden of St. Paul's Parish. In 1793 General Moultrie planted a crop of one hundred and fifty acres on Northampton plantation. This was a decided failure, the result of his unacquaintance with the proper method of culture.

The cotton culture from this time progressed rapidly in these parishes. This plant and indigo struggled against each other for the ascendancy. In three years the latter ceased to be grown as a market crop. To prove the value of the crop and the success of some of its planters in the parish, in

1799, Captain Peter Gaillard, of the Rocks plantation, averaged three hundred and forty dollars per
hand; and in the same year Captain James Sinkler,
at Belvidere, from a crop of three hundred acres,
realized the amount of two hundred and sixteen
pounds per acre, for much of which he received
seventy-five cents per pound, and for none less than
fifty cents—total, five hundred and nine dollars per
hand.   When first planted as a crop, various were
the modes adopted for its cultivation, both as to the
distance most proper and the amount of tillage
necessary.   The crop of Captain Gaillard above
alluded to was planted on hills four feet square, and
two stalks left in each hill.   Four workings were
deemed sufficient for making a crop: the first hoeing was invariably a flush or hoeing down process;
afterwards it was drawn up.   The seeds were universally planted in drills on the beds, which were
four feet apart and about their present size; the
thinning was done by careful hands selected from
the gang, doing daily three half acres the first and
four at the second thinning.

Peter Gaillard was born at the residence of his
father, at Wambaw, St. James' Parish, Santee, in
the year 1757, being the youngest of a family of five
sons and three daughters.   He and David were full
brothers, his father having a second time married
after the birth of the first six children.   The parents
were among the Huguenot emigrants from France

the year following the Edict of Nantes. Peter grew up to the age of ten before he was placed at school, and I have heard him say he believed the rapid progress he made was mainly owing to the shame and mortification he was subjected to by finding boys much his juniors in age his superiors in learning; he soon took a high stand in the school. When this school was discontinued, as there was a good one near Milford, my grandfather's residence in St. Stephen's Parish, he, together with Peter Robert, John Ball, and Francis Peyre, all cousins, were sent to that school under the charge of their uncle, Isaac Dubose, who had five children attending the school at the time, viz.: Isaac, David, Samuel, Catharine, and Joanna. After finishing their academic course here, Peter Gaillard and Samuel Dubose were sent to Charleston as clerks in the store of Theodore Gaillard, Peter's elder brother.

Here they continued until the war broke out. In consequence of the death of both David and his wife Joanna Dubose, Peter became owner of the White Plains plantation, to which he removed and lived with Samuel Dubose for some time as planters of indigo in the swamp. In the progress of events the two friends separated. Samuel Dubose taking side zealously with the Whigs, and the other remaining neutral. Most of the friends of Peter Gaillard warmly espoused the cause of the British government; and the violence and uncompromising character of his father probably influenced the son. Things remained so until the country got in the possession of the enemy. The British general, Cornwallis, called into the field most of those who had taken protection under his proclamation, and when a force was organized to hunt out Marion and his men on the Santee, Peter Gaillard was appointed second in command. General Marion, having ascertained the embodying and object of the party, suddenly fell upon them at Black Mingo and dispersed them; this was the only occasion where an active part was taken by Peter Gaillard against his countrymen. His friends had long known that he was lukewarm towards the cause he had espoused.

After his father's death Mr. Gaillard wrote a letter to my father, to the effect that his future services should be rendered for his country's success, and that if he could adopt means to have him introduced to Marion and his brigade, he would hold himself ready for any arrangement he could make, provided it involved no mortifying or humiliating feelings. An interview was forthwith had with General Marion, the subject opened, and the letter placed in his hands.

The General expressed heartfelt satisfaction at the announcement. He passed very warm encomiums upon Peter Gaillard's conduct at the battle of Black Mingo, stating that owing to circumstances the command devolved upon Peter Gaillard, who had gallantly sustained himself, and that if he had met with support from his brother officers the day would have been lost; Marion's force was the weakest, and he had hoped for a surprise, which he failed to effect. The horses' feet on the bridge a mile off apprised the sentinel of his approach, and allowed time for the enemy to prepare for the battle. Gen. Marion instructed my father to return his congratulations, and to say that at any hour fixed upon he would advance with his staff in front of his brigade, meet Mr. Gaillard as a friend, and escort him into camp. Policy dictated this, because Peter Gaillard had in the camp many bitter foes. The day after being fixed upon, my father, who was deputy brigade-major under Major K. Simons, left the camp, and returned with his friend at the point designated. As soon as he was in sight, Marion advanced with his staff, met and cordially greeted him, as did each of his family. The manner and the precautions taken thoroughly quashed every symptom of discontent. Peter Gaillard solicited and received posts of peril and honor in quick succession. When Col. Cotes fired Biggin Church and the large amount of stores contained in it, and attempted to reach Charleston by Bonneau's Ferry, Peter Gaillard was given a command to check him at Watboo and at Huger's bridges and at Bonneau's Ferry; this duty was gallantly performed, and the advance of the enemy stopped at " Brabant," the plantation of Bishop Smith. The Americans here came up, and Sumter, the senior officer, contrary to the earnest advice of Marion, rushed into a battle which proved disastrous to the Americans.

Mr. Gaillard was afterwards under the command of General Moultrie, and in many of the engagements south of Charleston. He also served under Col. John Laurens, was one of an advanced party to arrest the British in their retreat to Charleston, and witnessed the fall of Col. Laurens by one of the last balls discharged in that war.

After the war was over, Capt. Gaillard married Elizabeth Porcher, daughter of Peter, of Peru, a lady to whom he had long been attached. Some unpleasant and annoying occurrences he was fated to endure from a very few Whigs, who wanted magnanimity to cast a veil over his first and youthful error. His subsequent course appeared to produce no effect upon them. Death, however, in a few years, quieted every thing. And no man in any community ever commanded in a greater degree the confidence and esteem of his acquaintances, friends, and neighbors than did Capt. Gaillard.

I will add in corroboration, that in 1794, when the militia laws of the State were remodelled and the whole system changed, all commissions were vacated and new elections made. The parish unanimously elected him captain, and this at a time when commissions were more highly estimated than at present.

The disastrous ten years which preceded the introduction of cotton as a market crop involved him, as it did others, in debt and distress. His record book, kept with minute accuracy, states the fact, that in one of those years the entire crop saved from one of those freshets was a few baskets of unmatured corn, which required drying in the sun before it was fit for use. A family, and upwards of one hundred slaves, had to be sustained without money; credit had to be obtained from the more fortunate who planted on the Wateree or Congaree.

Capt. Gaillard purchased the Rocks in 1794, without funds, looking for nothing more than to make bread for his dependants. Cotton had not been attempted as a crop, and indigo did not pay for its cultivation. He settled the plantation in 1795, and made provisions. In the following year he attempted cotton, I believe over one hundred acres, with unlooked-for success. On my return from school in Camden, late in December, 1796, I called in to dine with his overseer, a friend of mine, and saw, for the first time, the process of ginning and specking cotton. A brilliant prospect now opened to the eyes of the desponding planters,

fully to be realized.   The crop of 1799 or 1800
extricated him from debt.   About twenty-two years
after, Capt. Gaillard divided his lands and negroes
among eight children, and retired in a green old
age to enjoy as much of the world's happiness as is
the lot of man, and lived ten years after.

I never knew a better, a neater, or a more successful planter than Capt. Gaillard.   There was a
completeness and finish, a compactness and uni-
formity about every thing, that was pleasant to the
eye.   In a ride one day to " Lifeland," my grandfather, Peter Sinkler, became the subject of conversation, and the captain thus expressed himself
about him as a planter.   " If you will make him,
Mr. Sinkler, the standard of a planter, I have never
known any other."   I adopt and apply this opinion
to him upon the maturest consideration.   There
was a generosity that belonged to him that few
possessed, and the knowledge of which would be
gratifying to his descendants.   When a rapid ac-
cumulation of funds in his factor's hands took
place, his nephew and factor, Theodore Gaillard,
Jr., borrowed of him a large sum of money, and
mortgaged for its safety the plantation now owned
by Thos. Ashby Esq., and a number of negroes.
After the bankruptcy of Mr. Gaillard, the mortgage foreclosed, the property sold for very little to
Captain Gaillard, owing to a great blunder of one
of the banks, which held a younger mortgage.

When the Captain found that half the purchase could pay him the bona-fide debt, and leave thirty negroes, he generously made it over to Theodore's children. When he married his second wife, he became entitled to her property, but he never used one cent of it, but gave it all to her children, returning even what she had used as his wife. In the twenty-three or twenty-four years after Capt. Gaillard had paid his last debt, he paid for real property $118,000 ; retaining for his own use upwards of $13,000 in stock, and dividing among his children upwards of five hundred negroes.

The gin first used for cleaning cotton of the seed was a clumsily constructed foot gin without the wheels, as now used, but instead, two cross-pieces with clubs at their ends, to give the necessary power. The greater part of the crops was either ginned early in the morning, or after task-work at night, a hand doing four or five pounds at each time. Cotton at that period, down to the introduction of the fine selected seed from the sea islands, invariably yielded one pound of clean to every three of seed cotton, and when seed was selected it was with the view of its so yielding. At that time, quantity and not quality was the aim in view ; consequently, heavier yields were obtained from our lands. Capt. Gaillard told me that his average of cotton on the Rocks, for twenty years, was one hundred and fifteen pounds per acre. My average at Ward's plantation for the six years (I planted it in coarse cotton) was one hundred and twenty-three pounds per acre, from the year 1850 to 1856 inclusive.

In the accounts current published in the gazettes of 1792 the article of cotton does not appear, yet it is evident that even at a much earlier date it was vended in Charleston in small parcels varying from one to thirty pounds. In 1787 two or three bags, about one hundred pounds each, were packed by Mr. S. Maverick and shipped to England as a sample and experiment. The answer of the consignees was discouraging. It is not worth producing, said they, as it cannot be separated from the seed.

In 1794 Col. Wm. Thomson, of revolutionary memory, planted cotton for market at Belleville, in St. Matthew's Parish. In 1796 cultivators of the crop appeared in several parts of the State. It was first grown in the district of Sumter by John Mayrant, in 1798. The year afterwards Gen. Wade Hampton introduced the plant into Richland district. With the energy and sagacity which distinguished him, he began his operations on an extensive scale, and from six hundred acres he gathered over six hundred bags. Although not the first to use Whitney's gin in South Carolina, he was the first who used water as the propelling power.

Sea island, or black-seed cotton began to be raised in Georgia in experimental quantities in

1786. The native place of the seed is believed to be Persia. The first bag exported from Georgia was grown on St. Simon's Island in the year 1788. The black-seed cotton region of the State is bounded on the north and northwest by a line a few miles south of the line that separates Barnwell and Orangeburg from the neighboring parishes; on the northeast and east by the Santee River, on the west and southwest by the Savannah River. It formerly was cultivated both in Williamsburg and Sumter districts, in their southern portions.

The crops were sufficiently encouraging, but the preparation of the wool was objectionable ; the growers abandoned the experiment on account of the large expenditure of labor and time that it required.

The first attempt in South Carolina to raise a crop of long cotton was made in 1788, by Mr. Kinsey Burden, of St. Paul's Parish. The product was packed in the article called Hessians. In 1780, when England had no fine manufactories, the best cottons brought to her market were from Demerara and Surinam. These then commanded about two shillings. These were superseded by the sea islands, which in 1799 sold readily at five shillings per pound. Its price in this State in the infancy of its production was generally from ninepence to two shillings, until 1806 or 1807, when for the first time

the planters experienced the baleful effects of re-
strictions on commerce.   From the superiority
of this cotton to that raised in any other country,
even from the same seed, the staple at first was
objected to as too long, and by one or two English
spinners it was actually cut shorter.

When first planted the seed was placed in small
hills five feet square, but by some in holes made on
the level land that distance apart. Seldom more than
one hundred pounds were made to the acre, until
the system of having more stalks in the acre was
adopted.   It may be remarked that the plough was
practically unknown to the first growers of long
cotton, and is still so here to a great extent, although
half a century has elapsed.

Notwithstanding the facilities offered by the
woods everywhere for an abundant store of suitable
aliment, no effort at manuring extended beyond a
potato field, which never exceeds a quarter of an
acre of land to the hand.   There were no rakes for
collecting leaves, nor carts specially designed for
carrying the vegetable offal to the cattle pen or
stable.

Various were the gins constructed for cleansing
the cotton of the seed.   The first was Eave's gin,
to be worked by animal or water-power; next,
Pottle's, of Georgia; Birnie's, Simpson's, and
Nicholson's gins; next, Whitmore's, Farris' and
Logan's. These were all modifications of Eave's

gin. None of these, however, stood the test of trial, and were successively abandoned for the foot-gin. Some of these gins were bought at two hundred and fifty dollars each. As slovenly as was originally the tillage of the cotton plant, the preparation of its produce for market was much more so. It was indeed so badly cleaned as to be deemed suitable only for the coarser fabrics.

Up to 1830, the pickers took no especial pains to abstract the dead leaves. The wool was sunned all day, and ginned often with stained particles incorporated with it. In the process of moting, these were removed by women sitting on the floor, where it was whipped with twigs. No bag or box received the cotton as it fell from the gin. In packing, an old iron axle-tree or wooden pestle was used, as at present. With many the cotton was ginned, moted, and packed in the same room.

It is proper here to remark that while the quality of the wool has been vastly improved, the product of the plant has been proportionately diminished. Although, therefore, the pecuniary circumstances of some individuals have been greatly improved, the planters generally have sustained a loss, in some instances to an almost ruinous extent. The stalk produces no more pods, and yet, five and often seven pounds of seed cotton are required to yield one of clean, instead of one to three, as formerly. Ten years ago, the staple of our sea

island cotton was about twenty per cent. better
than any other cotton produced ; owing to circumstances, it is now estimated at from thirty to forty
per cent. in favor of the former.[1]

Encouraged by the actual product of their fields,
our fathers continued to cultivate the grounds
which their judgments first selected for the new
crop.   After several years of exhausting tillage, it
became obvious that a radical change in their operations must take place.   Unaccustomed to receive
information from books concerning their pursuits,
the plain alternative of resorting to virgin soils
was adopted, and soon as one field was worn out
another was cleared.

In most beginnings, awkwardness and want of
skill retarded our full success.   In no case have I
known a more striking exemplification than in that
which I am about to relate.   To as late a period as
1801, to pack a bag of cotton was deemed a reasonable day's work, without the packer's having himself to make the bag.   This was considered a
seamstress's work, who found five an ample day's

---

[1] The value of cotton yarn is estimated by its length.   The extreme of
fineness, says Mr. Baines in his work on the "Cotton Manufactories of
Great Britain," published in 1835, to which yarns for muslins are even spun
in England, is two hundred and fifty hanks to the pound, which would yield
a thread measuring one hundred and nineteen and a half miles.   A pound
of fine cotton manufactured into the finest lace yields from four hundred
and eighty to five hundred hanks per pound, and makes a thread from one
hundred and ninety-seven to two hundred and thirty-eight miles long, and
is worth from sixty dollars to four hundred and fifty dollars per pound.

task. The overseer on Belvidere plantation pondered on this, and desirous of doing the community a service, sent an invitation to the gentlemen of Pineville to visit Belvidere to see his packer measure off three bags, make and pack them to hold three hundred and six pounds each, in time for them to return to Pineville in seasonable time,—and that they should be provided with as good a dinner as he could furnish. Strange to say, this invitation was not taken in good part by all. Mr. John Palmer alone accepted the call and determined to attend. On the appointed day he went up and witnessed the performance of the promise. On leaving one hour and a half before sunset, the third bag had only to be headed, and by seven o'clock the same evening the announcement was made to the gentlemen in Pineville. Thirty years after, I knew the same packer execute the same task, with ease to himself, when required.

At the time when planters relied altogether upon the swamp lands for their incomes, they were occasionally disappointed by the recurrence of freshets. To the most enterprising it occurred that embankments would effect some security, particularly against what would be called *small rises.* The Sinklers, Peter and James, took the lead in this, and to a degree were renumerated for their labor ; but the water surrounding their banks on all four sides allowed no possibility of getting off what rained in or soaked in through the banks. The experiment was therefore abandoned. Major Samuel Porcher, aware of the cause of the failure, and possessing a plantation which jutted against the high land, judiciously determined to avail himself of the advantage which circumstances afforded him, and for years kept his resolve to himself, until he was enabled to purchase some adjoining tracts of land which were essential to his success. At length this was accomplished, and in 1817 he commenced his great work. Few men are free from weak points of character, and most men can be made to act weakly if assailed at these points. Major Porcher, however, was not swayed by any adverse opinions, the advice of friends, or the laughter and jeers of others, but on he went, in a wonderful reliance on his own judgment. Who will not now admit that he has given greater evidence of practical wisdom, enterprise, persevering energy, patience, and indomitableness of purpose than any other South Carolinian? Any man in this country who can make his provisions in a rich swamp, and plant only long cotton on high land, every acre of which he can therefore manure, has it in his power to thrive, and need never think of the West.

Mr. Samuel Foxworth, then nineteen years of age, as his overseer, and his driver George, through a period of thirty years, served him faithfully. When the work was about to begin, George was

promised his freedom upon its completion ; the
promise was kept. It was a gratifying sight in
after time to see the old man living in close con-
tiguity to the scenes of his labor and anxieties,
enjoying the privileges he had won. And what
has bound Mr. Foxworth through the long period
of forty years to " Mexico," but the "bank"? Nothing else. For forty years he has been building a
great work, and repairing and improving it; he has
thought of it by day, and dreamed of it by night,
with the anxious solicitude that a mother feels for
her infant. At times he almost fainted and desisted
from despondency ; then again he worked with zeal
and enthusiasm inspired by hope. All the time he
labored in more or less doubt, whether the result
would be a blank or a prize ; and much of this time
he had to endure the ridicule of doubters. Whenever drawbacks or disasters occurred, and he had
to plunge into mud and water to repair damages
that seemed to yawn a warning mockery of his
power, instead of condolence and well-wishes of
his neighbors and friends, he received from the
enemies of the great work the taunting exclama-
tions: "I told you so." At length the "bank"
was completed, then perfected, and " Mexico " became the land of promises realized. The swamp
yielded in abundance its corn, oats, etc., and echoed
with the exultant bellowing of fat cattle, and the
once exhausted fields of high land, now devoted

exclusively to cotton and receiving a double amount of manure and rest, became more productive than nature had originally made them.

To whatever embarrassment and distress these parishes were subjected by the circumstances of the times, the districts of the upper portion of the State had their full share and even more. Rice and naval stores were out of their reach. Wheat, for the want of merchant mills, availed them little beyond their domestic wants. The first mill erected was in Camden, by Col. Broome, in 1795 ; the production of that grain was greatly stimulated thereby, and Camden soon became a market for flour of a superior quality. At the same time tobacco, as a market crop, was planted, chiefly by emigrants from Virginia. Extensive inspections were established, the first one near the bank of the Wateree River, but this with about two hundred hogsheads of tobacco was swept away by the unprecedented freshet of 1796. It was afterwards rebuilt in the town of Camden. The cultivation received an impetus, as well in that district as in some of the adjacent counties of North Carolina ; the business was pursued with considerable energy and success. To get the heavy hogshead to market, an axle was run through the centre and traces fixed to each end ; it was thus drawn or rolled by one horse to market, hundreds of miles.

But the curse which a seeming necessity had

brought upon the inhabitants was the business of manufacturing ardent spirits. The chief source of income from most of the farms was apples and peaches to supply the distilleries, which were dotted every three or more miles throughout the up country. Intemperance followed as a natural consequence, and demoralization afflicted society to a frightful degree. My residence in Camden about this time made me a witness of scenes degrading to the nature of man and revolting to the feelings. Imagine then the abandonment of these for a substitute like cotton. In cultivation easy, healthful, remunerative, and congenial to almost every acre of land in our wide-spread Southern and Western country. A labor in which wives and daughters may conveniently and safely share with the husband and father. While he traces the furrow, they, protected by their sun bonnets, eradicate the weeds with a light hoe.

A few years afterwards, independence and the peace of mind which it brings became their possession ; with these morality and good order improved, and in a short time cotton was acknowledged and hailed as a blessing from God to the human race. For clothing, for wealth, with abundance and cheapness of cloth, who can plead an excuse for want of supply and cleanliness ?

In casting our eyes over the prospect of our country, and reflecting upon the evils which occasionally beset us, do not the lessons of the past teach us the virtue of frugality and the necessity of a change in the relations which now exist between the factor and planter? The former should not incur obligations, startling in their amount and beyond their control, when monetary disturbances arise to distress them ; and the planter must not so heedlessly avail himself of accommodations so freely tendered. With cotton and sugar, rice and tobacco, necessary for the world's consumption, in the hands of the South, her influence would be paramount over every portion of the world. In vain is it that hundreds of thousands of fields grow white annually with the harvests, if creditors own it before it be gathered. If this goes on, the power placed in our hands will be barren, and we shall find ourselves in the hands of the domestic and foreign purchaser. The memory of one reverse should, it might be supposed, continue long enough to prevent the recurrence of old follies, or the repetition of former fatal mistakes. But it is a melancholy truth that almost utter forgetfulness of past suffering succeeds the dawn of prosperity, or if remembered at all they are no more than the visions of a disturbed sleep. Our labors suffer most from these monetary disturbances, whilst we are the factor's debtors ; but there would be no necessity for this if the planters were free from heavy pecuniary obligations to the factor. His marketable staples would not

lose their intrinsic value and fall a sacrifice in the
struggle. The indebtedness of the planter to the
factor, anticipating the proceeds of the crop, and
being one year in expenditures ahead of receipts,
has done more to produce the mischief than all
other causes combined. But for this our merchants
could have dictated the price of cotton to the con-
sumers of the world.

REMINISCENCES

OF

St. Stephen's Parish, Craven County

AND

NOTICES OF HER OLD HOMESTEADS

By SAMUEL DUBOSE

Printed at the Request of numerous Friends desirous of Preserving the fast fading History of that Interesting Region.

REMINISCENCES.

To Prof. F. A. Porcher.

My Dear Sir:—You request me, as the oldest inhabitant left among us, to give you of the present day as particular an account as I may have it in my power, of the individuals who once peopled this portion of our State, and as much of their habits, occupations, and genealogy as I either knew and remember, or have learnt from others. It is in compliance with this request that I have made the following sketch. I have often regretted that the opportunities for something better and more satisfactory had been so thoughtlessly neglected.

About twenty years before the revolutionary war, the belt of land bordering on the Santec River, through the whole extent of the parish of St. Stephen's, was the garden spot of South Carolina. The lands were not liable to the high and sudden freshets to which they have since been subject. The upper country being then but partially cleared and cultivated, the greater part of its surface was covered with leaves, the limbs and trunks of decaying trees, and various other impediments to the quick discharge of the rains which

fall upon it, into the creeks and ravines leading
into the river ; consequently much of the water
was absorbed by the earth or evaporated before it
could be received into its channels, and even when
there so many obstacles yet awaited its progress,
that heavy contributions were still levied upon it.
The river, too, had time to extend along its course
the first influx of water before that from more
remote tributary sources would reach it.   Owing
to these and other causes, the Santee was comparatively exempt from those freshets which have since
blighted the prosperity of what was once a second
Egypt. A breadth of three or four miles of swamp
as fertile as the slime of the Nile could have made
it, was safe for cultivation ; and its margins were
thickly lined with the residences of as prosperous a
people as ever enjoyed the blessings of God. Some
there were who lived in the swamp, and even on
the very bank of the river. The exceeding fertility
of the soil rendered labor scarcely necessary to
make it a wilderness of vegetable luxuriance. The
great quantity of decomposing matter, and the
myriads of insects incident thereto, and the abundant yield of seeds, furnished by the rank weeds
and grass, caused the poultry-yard to teem with a
well-fed population, and the pastures of crab grass
and cane, which are yet proverbial, poured into
the dairies streams of the richest milk, and enlivened the scene at morn and evening with the

lowing of herds of fat cattle. Nor were swine in abundance, and countless fish of the finest quality from the exhaustless river, wanting to fill up the measure of the people's comforts.

Before the eye was spread nature in all her majesty and beauty : here the noblest of American forest-trees in all the perfection which prosperity can develop ; there a noble placid river flowing in its slow majestic course, its opposite low and beachy shore fringed with the delicate willow whose branches drooped into the gliding current. On each side were seen nature and art co-operating to produce as rich a prospect as ever caused the eye of the agriculturist to dance with hope. I have never listened to representations of comfort more perfect and exuberant than those often given me of the scenes which I am attempting to describe, by those who had known and loved them. It was my delight, when a boy, to hear told how at evening the family would sit in the humble porch, and enjoy the rich delights of a spring twilight, listening to the songs of the feathered multitude, the stirring buzz of the bees as they carried their last load to their hives, the cackling of the poultry as they sought their proper resting-place, the sad wail of the whip-poorwill, the lowing of the richly freighted cows, and the bleating of their eager young, and admiring the rich and gorgeous colors of the trees, shrubs, and plants, varied according to their natures and the mellowing influence of the fading light. But the thoughts of that land of Goshen have caused me to linger by the way and to lose sight of the narrative I have promised.

Such was the country[1] that attracted the attention of so many of our Huguenot ancestors and induced them to abandon their first homes in St. James', Santee, and seek one so much more congenial to the indigo plant, at that time the staple product of the State, and made more profitable by the bounty granted by the mother country. One after another of the planters moved up as opportunity offered for the purchase of land, and in a very few years the population exceeded that of any other portion of the State out of Charleston. At the commencement of the revolution the militia company of St. Stephen's numbered one hundred and twenty-six men, rank and file, and the tax returns showed that there were five thousand slaves owned within the parish; and this, too, when the settlements were, with very few exceptions, north of the river road, and about half a dozen plantations on Fair Forest swamp.

1. The plantation known as "Mexico," at the western extremity of the parish, was the residence of the late Major Samuel Porcher. This plantation is made up of several small tracts of land, many of which had been the homesteads of their

[1] See Note A at the end.

owners. Major Porcher was the fourth child of
Peter Porcher of Peru. In 1789 he married Harriet, daughter of Philip Porcher, by whom he had a
daughter, Harriet, who married James Gaillard,
second son of Peter Gaillard of the Rocks ; and
three sons, Philip, who married Selina Shackelford,
Thomas William, who married the daughter of
Peter Gaillard, Jr., and W. Mazyck Porcher, the
present proprietor.

2. The next plantation was Burnt Savanna, now
a part of Belle Isle. For some time before the
revolution this place was the residence of General
Marion, and in its retirement he probably prepared
himself for the part he was to act in that stormy
period. He married late in life Mary Videau, and
died childless in 1795.

3. The third plantation, " Belle Isle," was the
residence of Robert Marion, Esq. He was the
third son of Gabriel Marion and Catharine Taylor.
His brothers, Gabriel and Benjamin, never married. Of his sisters, Catharine died unmarried ; his
younger sister, Charlotte, married Anthony Ashby,
by whom she had a daughter, who married Richard
Singleton, and after Mr. Ashby's death she married
Theodore S. Marion, by whom she had a daughter,
who, in 1808, became the wife of the writer. Mr.
Robert Marion married Mrs. Esther Deveaux (née
Gignilliat), mother of the late Stephen G. Deveaux.
This marriage produced no children.

4. Northwest of Mexico, and directly on the river bank, was the residence of Thomas Walter, Esq., the botanist, an Englishman by birth. He embellished his seat with a botanical garden, which long commanded the admiration of his neighbors. His first wife was Sarah Peyre, by whom he had two daughters ; his second wife was Dolly Cooper, whose daughter, Emily, their only child, married Judge Charlton of Savannah.

5. Between Belle Isle and the river road on the south was the residence of Peter Couturier. He married Rebecca Couturier, by whom he had a son, Elias, father of the late Peter Couturier. After his death his widow married Gideon Kirk, and became the mother of the late Mrs. Harriet Marion, of Robert Kirk, and of Louisa Kirk.

6. South of the road was the residence of Dr. James Lynah, a native of Ireland ; from this place he attended to a large medical practice. Both this place and that of Mr. Couturier now constitute a portion of Belle Isle.

7. Blueford was formerly the residence of Philip Williams, who, removing to York, sold it to Peter Sinkler. By him it was left to his son Peter, who, dying childless, bequeathed it to the children of his sister Elizabeth, wife of Samuel Dubose. It was the residence of the late Col. William Dubose, her second son, and is now that of Julius Dubose, his nephew and her grandson.

8. North of Blueford was Milford, the residence of Isaac Dubose, who left it to his eldest son, Isaac, by whom it was sold to Samuel Cordes. The elder Isaac Dubose married Miss Boisseau, by whom he had three sons and two daughters, viz. : Isaac, who married Mary Dutart ; David, who married Elizabeth Moncrieff ; and Samuel, who married Elizabeth Sinkler. His daughter Joanna married David Gaillard of White Plains ; his other daughter, Catharine, died unmarried.

9. The Lane plantation was owned by Samuel Cordes, Esq.

10. Tower Hill was settled by John Couturier. He married Elizabeth Couturier, and had three sons and a daughter. His son John married first a Miss Cook, and after her death Miss Ann Cahusac ; they were the parents of the late Dr. John Couturier of Pineville. Thomas married Miss Buford of Williamsburg, who, after his death, married Judge Richardson. Joseph married Miss Ellinor Couturier, and after her death Miss Louisa Kirk. The daughter married Major William Macdonald.

11. The Island was formerly a homestead, and when I first knew it, was the property of John Couturier. It is now a part of Tower Hill.

12. I do not know who first settled and occupied Johnsrun. It was once owned by the Williamses, who lived there ; it was held by various persons on

hire until 1793, when it was bought by a Frenchman, who soon abandoned it, and it was purchased by Capt. John Palmer. It is now the residence of his grandson, S. Warren Palmer.

13. Between this place and the river is Ray's, so called from the former owner and resident. He died about 1793.

14. On the east of Ray's was Claybank, the property and residence of Peter Palmer, and now a part of Richmond. In 1790 Mr. Palmer left this place for Pole Bridge, three miles to the south.

15. West of Pole Bridge is Murrell's, called by the name of the original owner; it passed into the hands of John Frierson, and was afterwards owned and settled by Samuel Dubose, son of Isaac, of Milford. Mr. Dubose married first Elizabeth, daughter of Peter Sinkler, and had four children, viz.: Samuel, who married Eliza Marion, and after her death Ann P. Stevens; William, who married Laura Stevens; Elizabeth, who married Colonel Thomas Porcher; and Anna Maria, wife of William Cain. After the death of Elizabeth Sinkler, Mr. Dubose married Mrs. Martha White, and had Isaac, who married Marianne Porcher; Martha, the wife of Peter Porcher of Tibbekudlaw; and Louisa, wife of David Gaillard, late of Fairfield.

16. Richmond was settled in 1769 by John Palmer, and was his residence until his death in 1817. He married Ann, the daughter of Robert

Cahusac, by whom he had three sons—John, who married Mary Jerman, Joseph, who married Eliza Porcher, and Maham, who died unmarried—and two daughters: Anne, the wife of O'Neal Gough Stevens, and after his death of Peter Gaillard, of the Rocks; and Marianne Gendron, wife of Gabriel Gignilliat, and afterwards of George Porcher.

17. South of Richmond was Maham's, the residence of Col. Hezekiah Maham. His wife was Miss Guerin; and they had two daughters, one of whom married Mr. Waties, and the other Dr. Haig. Both of these ladies became widows and married again—the first, Robert Smith; and the second, Dr. Samuel Wilson of Charleston.

18. Next to Richmond and east of it was the residence of Charles Richbourgh. He left no children, and the place was purchased by Theodore Gaillard of Charleston. It now forms a part of the Richmond tract.

19. Chinners was settled by a person of that name, and abandoned before the revolution. It is now part of Lifeland.

20. Next is Lifeland, the residence of Peter Sinkler. This place was purchased by his mother from Mrs. Jamison, who married Gen. Sumter. Peter Sinkler had a brother, and a sister, Dolly, who married General Richardson of Clarendon. Mr. Sinkler's first wife was Elizabeth Mouzon, sister of Henry Mouzon, the surveyor and engineer.

Their children were Jane, who married Joseph Glover, of Colleton ; Peter, who married Mary, daughter of Richard Walter ; James, who never married ; and Elizabeth, wife of Samuel Dubose of Murrell's.　His second wife was Miss Boisseau, who died childless.　His third wife was Catharine, daughter of Joseph Palmer of Webdo.　She had a daughter, Catharine, who married Francis Peyre. His fourth wife was the widow of René Peyre ; her daughter by her first husband, Florida Peyre, married John P. Richardson.

Few patriots of the revolution suffered more than Peter Sinkler, and as woe even if long continued is soon told, we shall dwell briefly upon his sufferings. His age, position, and strongly marked character gave him considerable influence with his fellow citizens ; and the British, who were aware of it, determined to get him in their power.　After many ineffectual attempts to take him, they succeeded by bribing his brother-in-law James Boisseau, an ingrate who betrayed the man that gave him a home.　Like most of the Whigs, Mr. Sinkler was accustomed occasionally to enjoy in the bosom of his family a respite from the fatigues and privations of Marion's camp.　Aware of the danger to which he was exposed, but totally unsuspicious of the person who was to betray him, he had a hiding-place in the swamp that lay not fifty yards north of his house, where he could be secure from everything but treachery. When he was known to be at Lifeland, Boisseau covertly introduced a party to his lurking place, and at the same time a party of the British approached the house by the avenue. As soon as this party was seen, Mr. Sinkler retired to his place of concealment and there found himself a captive. He was not allowed to take leave of his wife and daughters, but was carried to Charleston, a prisoner, without even a change of clothes, and thrust in the southeast cellar of the provost, now the post-office, where were others as unfortunate as himself, without bedding or even straw to lie upon. Typhus fever soon put an end to his sufferings.

He was detained at Lifeland long enough to witness the brutality of his captors and the savage recklessness with which they wantonly destroyed his property. The beds were taken from the house, ripped open, and their contents scattered to the winds ; his provision houses were opened and sacked, his poultry and stock shot down, and several crops of indigo destoyed or carried off. After his death a commission was appointed by the State to ascertain the amount and value of property so destroyed, and the following schedule was furnished by Capt. John Palmer : fifty-five negroes ; twenty thousand pounds of indigo ; sixteen blooded horses ; twenty-eight blooded mares and fillies ; one hundred and thirty head of stock cattle ; one hundred and fifty-four head of sheep ; two hundred hogs ; three thousand bushels of grain ; twenty thousand rails ; household furniture, liquors, plantation tools, poultry, etc., to the value of £2,500 currency. The reward of Boisseau's treachery was a commission in the British army and a civil station in Nova Scotia, which he enjoyed during his life.

21. On the east of Lifeland was the residence of a Mr. Seymour, who died or removed before my recollection. This place forms a part of Lifeland.

22. Windsor, the next plantation, was the residence of John Gaillard, Esq., who married Judith, daughter of René Peyre. They had three sons and four daughters. John, so long U. S. Senator, married Mary Lord, and had one son, the late Dr. Theodore Gaillard. Theodore, the late judge, married Cornelia Marshall ; Peyre married Miss Hall ; Elizabeth married Major Randall of the British army ; Mary married Dr. Samuel Thomas ; Lydia married Mr. Edward Croft ; and Louisa married Thomas Hunt, and had a numerous family now settled in Louisiana.

23. East of Windsor is White Plains, formerly the residence of David Gaillard, who married Joanna Dubose, and after his death, of Peter Gaillard of the Rocks, his younger brother. Peter Gaillard married Elizabeth, daughter of Peter Porcher of Peru. Their children were : first, Peter who married Eliza Gourdin ; second, Elizabeth, wife of John Stoney ; third, Lydia, wife of William Snowden ; fourth, James,

who married Harriet Porcher, and after her death
Henrietta Ravenel (née Gourdin), widow of Dr. ·
James Ravenel of Wantoot; fifth, Thomas, now of
Alabama, who married Marianne Palmer; sixth,
Catharine, wife of Thomas Porcher of Whitchall;
seventh, David, who married Elizabeth Palmer, and
after her death Louisa Dubose; eighth, Samuel,
who married Henrietta Palmer.

24. Ancrum's, the next place, was the residence
of Isaac Porcher. After his death his daughter
married George Ancrum, and they lived there till
death. Their son, William Ancrum, removed to
Camden, and sold the place to Theodore Gaillard,
who bequeathed it to his daughter Mrs. Theodore
Gourdin. It now belongs to her son, Capt. T. Louis
Gourdin.

25. Between Ancrum's and Peru reserve, a place
was inhabited by a Mr. Ray. I know no more of
him than his name.

26. Peru, the next place, was the residence of
Peter Porcher. He married Elizabeth Cordes, and
left four children: first, Elizabeth, wife of ·Peter
Gaillard of the Rocks; second, Peter, who married
Elizabeth, daughter of Benjamin Marion; third,
Thomas of Ophir, who married Charlotte Mazyck,
and after her death Elizabeth Dubose; fourth,
Samuel Porcher of Mexico, who married Harriet
Porcher.

27. The Oldfield plantation was the residence of

Philip Porcher, brother of Peter of Peru. His wife was Mary Mazyck. They had eight children : first, Mary, who died unmarried in 1834; second, Marianne, wife of Thomas Broughton of Mulberry; third, Philip, who married Catharine Cordes ; fourth, Peter, who married Charlotte Ravenel, and after her death Marion Johnston of Oakfield; fifth, Elizabeth, wife of William Mazyck, late of Charleston ; sixth, Harriet, wife of Major Samuel Porcher; seventh, George, who married Marianne Gignilliat (née Palmer) ; and eighth, Isaac, who married Mary, daughter of Plowden Weston, and after her death Mary, daughter of O'Neal Gough Stevens, and after her death Charlotte, daughter of René Ravenel of Pooshee. Mrs. Mazyck and Mrs. Porcher both died in 1843 ; they had lived with their husbands upwards of fifty-four years.

28. Dover, the next place, was formerly the residence of Robert Cahusac. It then became the property of Charles or Samuel Peyre, and after his death, of John Peyre, by whom it was sold to Philip Porcher. It was for several years the home of Isaac Porcher, and by him sold to Mrs. Charlotte Cordes.

29. East of Dover was Harleston's, so called from the name of the owner.

30. Yaughan, the next plantation, became, under the English law of primogeniture, the property of John Cordes. He generously surrendered it to his younger brother, Thomas Cordes, who lived and

died on it. His wife was Charlotte Evance, and their children were : first, the late Dr. Samuel Cordes ; second, Catharine ; third, Evance ; fourth, Lavidia, wife of C. B. Cochran, Esq.; fifth, Camilla. Mr. Cordes was an ardent patriot, and contrived to annoy the British in a variety of ways while they held possession of the parish. He would liberate their prisoners, delude them with false informations, break his parole, and made himself so obnoxious that it was determined to destroy him. A rope was put around his neck, and he was led to a large oak, on the very spot where the new road turns off, south of the Tavern bridge, when he begged as a last favor, to be allowed time to indulge in the luxury of smoking a pipe. It was granted, and before the pipe was finished a pardon opportunely arrived from Lord Cornwallis, who yielded to the entreaties of Theodore Gaillard, Mr. Cordes' brother-in-law, whose plantation was at the time the General's head-quarters.

31. Curriboo was the residence of Thomas Cordes, son of Samuel. He married Rebecca Jamieson, and left two children : James, who married the daughter of Jonathan Lucas, and went to live in England ; and Elizabeth, wife of the late Col. John Harleston.

32. Upton was the residence of John Cordes, who married Miss Banberry and left two children : Catharine, wife of the late Dr. Philip Prioleau ; and William, who died unmarried. After the death

of his wife, Mr. Cordes married Catharine Mazyck
of Woodboo. He became the owner of Peru, and
resided there until his death.

33. Sandyhill was formerly the residence of René
Richbourgh. He had two daughters: Elizabeth,
wife of Thomas Palmer of Grave Hill, who left two
children—Thomas, who died single; and Marianne,
wife of Thomas Gaillard of Alabama. Catharine,
Mr. Richbourgh's second daughter, married O'Neal
Gough Stevens. Their children were: Charles, who
married Susan, daughter of René Ravenel of Pooshee; Catharine, wife of Dr. Henry Ravenel; and
Mary, wife of Isaac Porcher. Mr. O. G. Stevens,
after his wife's death, married Anne Palmer, by
whom he had two daughters: Anne Palmer, second
wife of Samuel Dubose; and Laura, wife of William
Dubose.

34. Next is the Parsonage, owned by the Episcopal church of the parish, and formerly the residence of the rector. It has long been without a
house.

35. East of the Parsonage was the residence of
Zachariah Villepontoux. His wife was a Miss
Baird. They left no family.

36. The next place was the residence of Charles
Cantey, Jr., who married Margaret Evance, by
whom he had two daughters: Margaret, wife of
Press M. Smith; and Susan, wife of John Dubose.
Mr. Cantey died in 1789, and his widow survived

until 1848. She was for several years the " oldèst inhabitant," and her age, her cordial manners, her attachment to her home and her friends, the kindly interest she took in the welfare of all within her reach, the unaffected simplicity of her manners, her exhaustless fund of anecdotes of old times, and the sterling worth of her character endeared her to all who knew her, and caused her to be loved and respected in life, and unaffectedly lamented in death.

She retained to the last the primitive habits of her youth. Breakfast at or before sunrise, dinner by half-past twelve, tea before sunset, and supper to crown the labors of the day. She celebrated her birthday, which was in July, by an old-fashioned tea-party, to which everybody in her village was invited ; and on those occasions no business short of absolute urgency would ever prevent any planter from making it a point to return home early, to be in time for Mrs. Cantey's tea. It was a pleasure to pay her such attentions, for she knew with what spirit they were offered, and the warmth of her heart caused her to magnify their importance.

37. The next plantation was the homestead of Harriet, widow of Richard Walter, merchant of Charleston. She was the daughter of Charles Cantey of Mattesee, and her children were : Mary, wife of Peter Sinkler, Jr. ; Harriet, wife of Sims Lequeux ; Martha, wife of O. G. White, and after his death, of Samuel Dubose ; Sarah, wife of Ben-

jamin Joor ; Richard, who married Ellen Ford ; and John, who married Magdalen Taylor.

38. East of Mattesee Creek is Mattesee, the residence of Charles Cantey. His wife was a daughter of John Drake, and his son, Charles Cantey, married Margaret Evance. His daughter Sarah married James Sinkler, brother of Peter Sinkler of Lifeland, and after her death her sister Margaret became his second wife. Mary married John Peyre ; Harriet married Richard Walter ; Anne married René Peyre, and after his death, Peter Sinkler of Lifeland ; Charlotte married Benjamin Walker. Mattesee was afterwards the residence of Charles, only son of John Drake. He married Louisa Lequeux, and was the father of Mrs. Maria Snowden of Townhill.

39. Next to Mattesee was Lequeux's, so called from the owner's name. I remember nothing about his family.

40. Old Santee, the next plantation, was the residence of Captain James Sinkler. He married Miss Cahusac, and after her death Sarah, daughter of Charles Cantey, of Mattesee ; their daughter married J. B. Richardson. His third wife was Margaret Cantey, sister of his second. The issue of this marriage were : Charles, who married Elizabeth Peyre, and died childless ; William, who married Eliza, daughter of Archibald Brown ; and Anna, wife of John Thomson, of Belleville.

41. Betaw was the residence of Thomas Hasell Thomas. His wife was Anne, daughter of Thomas Walter, the botanist, and their children were : Dr. John Thomas, now of Fairfield, who married Harriet, daughter of Elias Couturier ; T. Walter Thomas, late of Abbeville, who married Elizabeth Kirk ; Edward, a minister of the Episcopal Church, whose wife was Jane, daughter of Judge Gaillard ; Hasell Thomas, who died unmarried ; Samuel Peyre Thomas, late of Fairfield, who married Jane Roseborough ; Anna, the only daughter, died unmarried.

42. Laurel Hill was the residence of John Peyre, who married Mary, daughter of Charles Cantey of Mattesee. No child survived their union. The place was sold to Captain Peter Gaillard of the Rocks.

Mr. Peyre, like many of his neighbors and friends, was a neutral in the contest with the mother country until after the fall of Charleston, when the proclamation was issued, in violation of the capitulation, calling on the people to bear arms in support of the king. Mr. Peyre obeyed the call, and was one of a strong party of Tories who had assembled at Black Mingo in Williamsburg District. Marion determined, with his usual activity, to break up this camp, and accordingly having left his post on the Peedee, he travelled forty miles in one day, attacked, defeated, and dispersed the party. Mr. Peyre and his brother Charles were taken prisoners. They were sent on foot to Philadelphia, and there kept in close confinement for eighteen months, during which time Mr. Charles Peyre died. On being released from captivity, Mr. Peyre found himself a stranger, in a strange place, in absolute want. A Quaker noticed him in the street, and, struck with something in his appearance, stopped and inquired into his situation. On hearing his story he handed him a purse containing funds amply sufficient to supply his wants and carry him home. Mr. Peyre gratefully and eagerly inquired who his benefactor was, so that he might requite his kindness; but the Quaker would not satisfy him. "Friend," said he, "I must not tell thee my name, and thou shalt never know me; all I ask in return is this: when thou meetest a fellow-sufferer, do likewise, and give as thou hast received." Mr. Peyre, who had seen his brother die in the prison, found on his return to Carolina that his sister, Mrs. Walter, was dead and her husband already again a married man; and the whole of his ample fortune was in the hands of a commission of sequestration under the authority of the State. With a few exceptions, the confiscated estates were generally restored to their owners. In this noble work of pacification none labored more zealously than General Marion.

43. Cooper's, so called from the resident, Thomas Cooper. His wife was Jane Harvey. Their daughter was the wife of David, son of Charles Gaillard. Their son Thomas died unmarried; Maurice mar-

ried Lydia, daughter of Samuel Lequex ; Charles married Louisa Whitfield ; James died unmarried.

44. Webdo was the residence of Joseph Palmer. He had one daughter who became the wife of Peter Sinkler, and whose daughter Catharine was the wife of Francis Peyre.

Between Webdo and the parish line lived the families of Dutarque, Guerry, Bisseau, etc., all of Huguenot stock, but of whose intermarriages and descendants I am unable to give any account.

The Fair Forrest Swamp is one of the principal feeders of the western branch of Cooper River, into which it flows through Watboo Creek. It rises in the bays within a few miles of Santee Swamp, and once afforded those who lived on its banks rice fields, which were precarious on account of their liability to freshets. Bordered on either side by a wide extent of pine forest, and in its whole length within a convenient distance of Watboo landing, the planters on this swamp had their attention early directed to the preparation of naval stores of all kinds, the prices of which were stimulated by the bounties paid by Great Britain for their exportation. The vicinity of this swamp therefore was the busy scene of this department of activity, and nowhere, perhaps, have labor and enterprise ever been so richly rewarded.

45. Beginning at the head of the swamp, the first settlement was the residence of Benjamin Walker.

His wife was Charlotte, daughter of Charles Cantey of Mattesee. Their daughter Ann married George English of Clarendon.

46. Tucker's, the next plantation, was the residence of the father of Peter and James Sinkler; after his death the family moved to Lifeland. As an instance of the facility with which property was accumulated at that time, it may be stated that on Mr. Sinkler's death his widow was left in possession of one male slave. When Peter Sinkler died, and he did not pass beyond the meridian of life, he left three plantations and several hundred negroes, besides the large amount of property of which he was plundered when taken prisoner by the British. His brother James was no less successful.

47. Gravel Hill was the residence of John Palmer, a gentleman whose successful enterprise in the collection of naval stores has caused him to be remembered in our days by the distinguished appellation of Turpentine John Palmer. His wife was Marianne, daughter of John Gendron, whose father, an emigrant Huguenot, was one of the pillars of the Church at Jamestown. Their children were: Capt. John Palmer, of Richmond, who married Anne Cahusac; Peter, who lived afterwards at Polebridge, and never married; and Thomas, who lived at Gravel Hill and married Elizabeth Richbourgh; after her death he married Amelia Jerman, and after her death, her sister, Harriet Jerman.

Age and the infirmity of gout prevented both Mr. John Palmer and his brother Joseph, of Webdo, from bearing arms during the revolutionary struggle. But the former had sons who were active Whigs, and the latter was known to be friendly to their cause. They were, therefore, made the victims of cruelty so wanton that it can hardly be credible that it proceeded from a civilized enemy. They were both seized and carried to Biggin Church, which was then a British post, and there inhumanly thrust into the Colleton family vault, without even a blanket to protect them from the unwholesome damps of their gloomy prison. After they were liberated they were two days returning to Gravel Hill, about ten miles distant. Oppressed with pain, infirmity, and anxiety, each brother occasionally carried the other on his back, when strength had failed and the urgency of advancing became or seemed apparent.

48. East of Gravel Hill was Cooper's, so called from a former resident. The place was afterwards a part of the Gravel Hill tract.

49. On Wiskinboo Swamp, a tributary of the Fair Forrest, was the residence of Mr. Edward Greenland, grandfather of William Cain, Esq. His daughter married Robert Cahusac, and was the mother of John, who married Eliza Williams ; of Anne, wife of John Couturier, the father of the late Dr. John Couturier of Pineville ; and of Susan,

who married Col. Robert McKelvey. After Mr.
Cahusac's death, his widow married Daniel Cain,
by whom she had two sons, Daniel and William
Cain.

50. West of the swamp, and opposite Gravel Hill,
was the residence of —— Boisseau, and afterwards
of Mrs. Lehre.

51. Spring Grove was the residence of René
Peyre. He was twice married. René Peyre's first
wife was Ann Cantey, sister of Mrs. John Peyre,
who married Peter Sinkler afterwards. His second
wife, Hannah Simmons, was the mother of Francis
Peyre, and of Anne, who married Thomas Ashby.
Francis Peyre, who succeeded his father on this
place, married Catharine, daughter of Peter Sinkler,
of Lifeland. Their children were : Elizabeth, who
married Charles Sinkler, and after his death, Thomas
Ashby ; Anne, the wife of Stephen G. Deveaux ;
Catharine, wife of Dr. Theodore Gaillard ; Florida,
wife of Isaac M. Dwight. Their son Francis married Mary, daughter of Col. Thomas Porcher of
Ophir. After Mrs. Peyre's death, Mr. Peyre married Mary Peyre, daughter of Thomas Walter, the
botanist. Their children were : Isabella, who married Dr. William Porcher ; Thomas Walter and
Hannah Ashby, both of whom died unmarried.

Thomas Walter Peyre succeeded his father as
proprietor of Spring Grove, and resided on it for
some years ; he afterwards removed to Brunswick,

in St. John's, and spent his summers in Pinopolis in the same parish, where he died in 1851. His virtues were celebrated in the sketch of Craven County, published in the *Southern Quarterly Review*, and I shall not dwell on them here. With him died the name of Peyre. The descendants of that once numerous and respected family exist only in the female line. His plantation is now owned by H. R. Banks, Esq., of Charleston.

52. South of Spring Grove was the residence of Pierre Robert, Esq., who never married.

53. The last plantation to be named in St. Stephen's Parish is LeBois, formerly the residence of —— Pinckney, and afterwards of Peter Porcher, son of Philip, and father of Dr. Peter Porcher of Charleston.

Besides the swamp lands, the margin of Biggin Swamp abounds in fertile land, and it was early taken possession of by a dense population, chiefly Huguenot, who cultivated indigo. These were principally the St. Juliens, Marions, Mazycks, Ravenels, etc., and their descendants still retain the greater part of these valuable lands. It is said that the St. Julien family consisted once of nine brothers, only one of whom married. His two daughters married : the one, General Moultrie ; and the other, Daniel Ravenel of Somerton. This name, like that of Peyre, has perished, and the blood subsists only in the female line.

A feature characteristic of this country, and one that deserves notice, is the family burying-grounds. After the erection of the St. Stephen's Church, the ground about it was the common cemetery, but many persons to this day continue to bury their dead in the old homestead, and chose to lie in death within the precincts of their ancestors' domain, even though perhaps they may have been strangers to it in life. The graveyard was near the house, usually behind the garden. As a precaution against the depredation of wolves, a large hole was dug to the depth of about five feet; a grave was then dug at the bottom of this hole, large enough to hold the coffin. After the coffin was deposited in this receptacle, it was covered with boards, and the whole then filled up. This practice continues to this day. I can hardly enumerate the several graveyards. Those which have been latest used are : that at Belle Isle, for the Marions and their descendants ; at Mahams, for the descendants of Col. Maham ; at the Old Field, for the family of Philip Porcher ; at Gravel Hill, for the Palmers ; at Hanover in St. John's, for the descendants of the St. Juliens ; and those at Pooshee and Somerton, for the families of the Ravenels and Mazycks. It is not unlikely that there are graves on almost every old homestead in the country.

Black Oak is the central point in a region interesting for various incidents connected with the revolution. These are too unimportant to have found a place in history; but we are near Eutaw and Quinby; we are on the highway that led from Charleston to nearly all the scenes where great deeds were performed; the armies of both friend and foe camped near us, and marched near us, and the people who lived in those days had countless incidents to relate, all of which possessed a local or an individual interest, and I cannot but regret that their memory has perished. None of the witnesses of these scenes survive, or if any linger still, he has long passed the limit allotted by the Creator as the period of human life. Would it not have been well had our Legislature appointed commissioners whose duty it should have been to collect and preserve authentic anecdotes which could have been furnished by those witnesses? The expense would have been trifling, and when once sustained would have been ever available in preserving from oblivion much of local interest, which would have been valuable to posterity. We are in the midst of sacred territory; about us armies were encamped, houses were burned, men imprisoned and brutally murdered; but as these were merely incidents to more stirring and important events, they have escaped the notice of the historian, and we now tread the ground without a thought of the scenes that were enacted upon it.

And not our own men only, but even our foes can

furnish incidents both pleasant and painful to remember. Not two miles from Black Oak, by the
roadside is seen the grave of Major John Majori-
banks. This officer was one of the most useful
and efficient of the British army at Eutaw. Having
under his command a flank battalion of infantry,
posted on the creek, he rescued victory from our
grasp when the day seemed fairly and completely
ours. The heat and the fatigues of that day, and
the unwholesome condition of the climate at that
season, gave him a fever. The British army (after
the worse than barren victory at Eutaw) was retreat-
ing to Charleston, now become their only place of
safety, and his comrades were forced to leave him at
Wantoot. Here, in the hut of a slave, this hero,
who but a fortnight before had saved the army of
his sovereign, now spent with disease, deprived of
all comforts, without hope and without sympathy,
lay, dependent on the slave of one against whom he
was waging a cruel war for all the assistance that
his situation required ; and in this humble hut he
sank, unwept and unknown, into the arms of death.
His remains received more honor from the Ravenel
family than from his comrades and associates. The
grave was long distinguished from the woody wilderness around it by a head-board, fashioned out of
a cypress plank lying about the plantation, the remains of an indigo vat. This head-board with its
inscription remained in its place until 1836, and

everybody admired the durability of the stuff which
had so long resisted the elements. In that year it
fell, and its place was immediately supplied by a
marble slab, erected by the sons of Daniel Ravenel,
who had planted the cypress head-board. Majori-
bank's fate was that of the soldier ; but yet, as we
view his lonely grave, and remember his high character and his unhappy end, we cannot but sigh at
the extinction of bright and ambitious hopes, nor
refuse our sympathies to the memory of a brave
man, whose spirit was yielded, unsolaced by a
mother's, a wife's, or a sister's ministering hand ;
whose grave was moistened by no tear shed by any
one who loved him.

Some distance beyond the St. Stephen's line, and
just below the Eutaw Spring, was another settlement, chiefly of Huguenot families,viz. : the Couturiers, Marions, Gignilliats, Chouvenaus, Gourdins,
etc., besides others of English descent, the McKelveys, Ervines, Olivers, Kirks, etc. All of these
in the course of time were connected by intermarriage. The land was well adapted to the growth of
provisions and indigo, and in consequence of the
fertility of the high lands they escaped the full
measure of the calamities with which their neighbors
of St. Stephen's were visited when the river became
unsafe. The same picture of a prosperous and happy condition with which I have introduced this sketch,
may be applied to this neighborhood also, and the

happiness which is there described, continued to be the portion of the people, until in the course of the revolutionary war the British got possession of the State, and established their military posts over every portion of the country. Then the people became more clearly divided into Whigs and Tories ; and their misery was increased by the proclamation of the British commander, offering to all who would accept it, peace and protection ; and complete exemption from the obligation of taking up arms against their countrymen.

Not only the Tories but even some of the most zealous Whigs accepted this delusive protection. With the exception of Marion and his handful of men, resistance had ceased to be entertained, and the State lay prostrate at the mercy of the conquerors.[1] Some of the most sagacious Whigs refused to be deluded by the bait, and when a brief period of repose exposed the hollowness of the protection, they again took up arms and abandoned the cultivation of their lands except for necessary provisions. Their ingenuity was also taxed to conceal their slaves and secure them from the avaricious clutches of their foes. When peace was restored every planter was in debt ; no market crops had been made for years ; and where the river swamp was their sole dependence, even provisions had not been made. It was not a season therefore merely of embarrassment ;

[1] See Note B., at the end.

ruin stared many in the face. Besides, with the exception of rice the country had no staple crop ; for since the bounty, which as colonists they had enjoyed on the export of indigo and naval stores, had been discontinued, these products ceased to have any value, and negroes fell in price. Prime gangs were not unfrequently sold for less than two hundred dollars per head.

I cannot better illustrate the total depreciation of value than by the following case : Milford plantation, consisting of one hundred acres of high land, and between three hundred and four hundred acres of swamp, had been purchased by Mr. Samuel Cordes for six thousand guineas sterling, and at the period of which I now write, was abandoned as worthless. To add to the other causes of distress, those whose property consisted in paper and securities were either not paid at all, or paid in valueless continental money. The people however had gained the great object of their years of toil, and they were sanguine respecting the future. Without relaxation of effort however poorly requited, they were sustained by the buoyant and elastic trait of the Huguenot character ; they had seen hardships before, and did not sink under these. They strove to reduce their expenses to the lowest possible point ; they manufactured clothing for themselves and their slaves ; raised abundant supplies of poultry and stock of various kinds, and with these contrived to live in plenty. The

bitter feelings generated by the war gradually soft-
ened down ; hostile families were reconciled, and the
intermarriage of their children formed a bond of
friendship.

After nearly ten years of unrequited labor, the
Santee Canal was projected, and constructed within
their neighborhood.   Every one availed himself to
a greater or less extent of this opportunity of hiring
their negroes ; for men they received thirty and for
women twenty pounds sterling per annum, besides
their food.   At times a thousand laborers were employed on this work, which was seven years in being
completed.   This enterprise, which was disastrous
to those who had embarked in it, rescued a large
number of planters from ruin.   It was commenced
in 1792, and finished in 1800.   Two or three years
after it had been commenced, a few planters in the
neighborhood tried the cultivation of cotton on a
small scale, but the progress of this enterprise was
slow and irresolute, in consequence of the difficulty
of preparing it for market.   With the improvement
of the gins, the cotton culture increased and was extended, until 1799, when Capt. James Sinkler planted
three hundred acres at his plantation Belvidere, on
Eutaw Creek, and reaped from each acre two hundred and sixteen pounds, which he sold for from fifty
to seventy-five cents per pound.   Since that period
no other agricultural staple has stood in the way of
its cultivation.

Dancing is a recreation in which our people have always indulged. The sports of the turf were eagerly enjoyed, and our fathers were fond of the most manly of all others, the ball alley. Before and some time after the war, there was an alley near the road by Blueford, which was attended by persons from every part of the State. General Sumter was often there, and he was unrivalled as a ball-player. Barbecues were favorite amusements, and always gave occasions for dancing. A certain number of families would by turn furnish these dinners at some convenient spot affording water as well as shade. The attendance would be general, and after the pleasures of the turf-spread table were over, those who were inclined to dance would retire to the house of some individual near by, and the night, and not unfrequently the following day, would be spent in dancing, the partners being engaged, not as now, for the half hour, but for the season. I can well remember the scenes of these barbecues, and the preparations for the dinner. The spots on which these festivals were held long continued to give unquestionable evidence of the scenes which had been enacted on them.

I feel loath to leave untold a story I have often heard in my youth of two young men, Daniel McKelvey and his cousin Robert, better known as Col. McKelvey, and father of the late Colonel.

A short distance below Eutaw Creek, on the

river bank, was the residence of a widow lady, whose only companion was an orphan girl, and whose property consisted of a small tract of land and a few negroes. Her neighbors were not remote, but the troubled state of the times and the difficulty of access to her dwelling in the swamp had, ever since the occupation of the country by the British, and the broad distinction now existing between Whigs and Tories, cut her off almost entirely from society. The brutality of the British and Tories in sacking houses, carrying off cattle, abducting slaves, insulting the defenceless, and sometimes burning the dwellings of those who were particularly obnoxious to them, was such as to prove that security was cheaply bought, even at the cost of the deprivation of society. A few, however, would occasionally seek the hospitality of her roof, among whom were the cousins McKelvey, who would fly from the toils and privations of the continental army to recruit in this garden of peace and of plenty. They were young men of fine talents, good connections, and easy fortunes. Robert was witty, humorous, and lively; Daniel, sober, sensitive, and of bland and amiable manners.

Seated in this retreat, at a table well spread indeed, but which to the ill-fed partisans appeared a display of prodigality, they were startled by a terrified negro rushing in with the alarming information that the redcoats were approaching through the cornfield, and were then within fifty yards of the house. The two McKelveys sprang through the back window to the ground, and dashed with the speed of hope, goaded by the love of liberty and life, to the river in the rear of the yard.

But nothing is swifter than the instrument of malice, or more circumspect than its foresight. Several muskets were fired in quick succession, and Daniel McKelvey fell. Robert continued his flight, reached the river bank unhurt by the volley of balls which flew about him, and plunged in. The channel, which lay far beneath the bluff, bore upon the bank, and had worn in it a crescent-shaped excavation. The pursuers were almost instantly on the bluff. They were eight or ten English soldiers, conducted by some Tories, of whom the leader was one Raburn, who had been in the employment of one of the McKelveys as an overseer. Raburn knew that McKelvey could not swim ; and as he communicated this information to his comrades, they left him to his fate. They carried Daniel, who was mortally wounded, into the house, and there, regardless of the tears and entreaties of the widow and orphan, proceeded to plunder. After having finished his arrangements for taking off slaves, horses, cattle, and whatever provisions could be transported in the plantation carts, Raburn turned to McKelvey and said : " I am going now, Daniel, and shall probably never see you again. Will you shake hands ? I have nothing against you, but that you are a d—d rebel." The victim was past speaking ; but he slowly placed his hand in that of his murderer, exhibiting in his last action the power of the Christian principle, and stamping with the seal of perfection a character which had always been lovely.

It was past midnight, and the two unhappy women were still hovering by the side of the dying McKelvey, when the door opened, and Robert McKelvey gently approached the mourning group. A glance of recognition brightened the eye of the sufferer, and was directly succeeded by the insensibility of death. When Robert McKelvey, who could not swim, had cast himself into the river, the current had borne him to the crescent-shaped excavation of the bank already mentioned ; and there a tree, whose foundation had been washed away, still floated, attached by a few roots to the earth. Getting under this tree, and clinging to it with his hands, its leaves and branches hid him from observation ; and in this retreat he lay until in the silence of night he ventured to come out and witness the havoc which his ruthless enemies had made.

Few of us are able to appreciate the sacrifices endured and the heroic resolution exhibited by our mothers of the revolution. True, the pen of the historian has often attempted to do them justice ; but only a few heroic and melodramatic acts can find their way into the pages of history. No pen can adequately describe the anguish of mind constantly endured for the fate of husbands and sons, exposed not merely to the dangers of the tented field, but to all the horrors of a civil war, in which life was every moment in peril from every quarter. It would be an endless tale to recount the instances of barbarous rudeness which they experienced from a remorseless and an exasperated soldiery, whose discipline was purposely relaxed by the stern policy of our unrelenting foe. No one can adequately portray those heartrending troubles which afflicted the lonely and isolated mothers with their tender offspring to support, not secure that even the meal in actual preparation would appease their craving appetites, for even this was often the prey of the robber soldier. Even the aid of servants was uncertain ; for no one could foresee the moment when it would be necessary to conceal them from his avaricious grasp. All these trials were endured with fortitude which none but women can exhibit. Often in childhood have I hung upon a mother's lap and listened with astonished wonder to the recital of tales of misery like these. Information from the camp was seldom received, and was always uncertain. The ladies adopted a system of telegraphing, by which it was extended as soon as it reached one of them. Flags were raised upon a pole, which by their shape and color indicated the character of the news as good or bad ; and as the houses were generally in sight one of the other, the news was quickly transmitted through the neighborhood.

The culture of the indigo plant was the principal occupation of the planters ; and its manufacture, or the process of extracting the dye, involved much risk and demanded, during the whole period of the process (the " making season " as it used to be called), not only skill, but unremitting attention. I can well remember how often, in the process of what was called " beating," the liquor was taken up in a plate and anxiously examined in the rays of the sun, in order to ascertain whether all the particles of dye were separated ; for, if not, the result would be a failure ; the bright true-blue color would not be obtained, and the value of the drug would be impaired. There were, as might be expected, many grades of professional reputation among the planters. I have often heard it said that, during the manufacturing season, Mr. Peter Sinkler would be three weeks without seeing his wife, though he slept every night in his bed. He would come home late at night, when she was asleep, and would return to the scene of his professional labors before she awoke in the early morning.

The process of culture and the manufacture, once so important to the people of this State, is now forgotten ; even Drayton, whose " View of Carolina "

was published in 1802, did not think it worth the
labor of description. As I saw the process habitu-
ally when a boy, and continued long to associate
with those who were engaged in its culture, I shall
briefly describe the whole process from the planting
of the seed to its departure from the plantation.

The land was well cleared, drained, and thoroughly broken up and pulverized ; after all apprehension of frost was over, the fields were laid off in
drills about an inch deep, and from twelve to fifteen
inches apart from each other. In these drills the
seeds, mixed with lime and ashes, were sown. If
the season was a fair one, the seeds came up within
ten days or a fortnight, and grew off rapidly. The
plants were cut three or four times in the season,
for making the dye ; and during all this period they
required nice and frequently repeated hoeing and
weeding. When they had grown to the height of
two or three feet, the plants were cut with a reaping
hook, and carried to the macerating vat. This vat
was strongly constructed of thick cypress planks,
raised some height above the ground. When this
vat, which was called the "steeper," was furnished
with a sufficient quantity of weed, clear water was
poured into it, and the weeds were left to steep or
macerate until all the coloring matter was extracted
from them ; the fluid was then drawn off by means
of a faucet into an adjoining vat called the " beater."
An axle to which were attached arms long enough

nearly to reach the opposite sides of the vat, and each furnished with a small bucket at its end, ran lengthwise through the centre of this vat. Laborers would then place themselves upon this vat, and work the axle with handles or cranks, so as to cause the buckets to rise and fall alternately in the liquor. This process was continued until the coloring matter was united in a body. This operation required great nicety, for if the beating was not continued long enough, a part of the tingeing matter remained dissolved in the liquor ; if continued too long, a part of that which had separated is dissolved afresh. Lime was then applied, which assisted in the separation of the water from the indigo. The whole being now suffered to rest until the blue matter had settled, the clear water was drawn off by cocks in the sides at different heights, and the blue part discharged by a cock in the bottom into another vat. It was then strained through cloth bags, and spread out in shallow vessels called " bowls," to harden and dry. When the substance had acquired sufficient consistency, it was cut into cakes or lumps, each weighing about one quarter of a pound. While packing the indigo for market, these lumps were brushed to make them as bright as possible. They were generally packed in bags or boxes.

Few planters attempted to cultivate more than four acres of indigo to the hand. The great enemy of the growing crop was the grasshopper, which would sometimes destroy the crop in a few days. The best remedy against this enemy was chickens. I recollect that my father was in the habit every year of sending into the swamp fields several hundred chickens ; movable coops were furnished for their accommodation at night, but no food ; nor did they require any so long as the grasshopper infested the fields. Those who could not use chickens suffered the margins of their fields to grow up in grass ; the grasshoppers, driven from the fields with whipping brushes, would alight in the grass, which was then fired in several places at once. The price of indigo varied at from a dollar to two dollars and a half per pound. Few planters ever realized more than one hundred and twenty dollars to the hand. The bounty allowed by the British government was sixpence sterling per pound.

The culture of indigo and its manufacture is said to be attended in the West Indies and in other parts of the world with diseases, violent, severe, and at times fatal. If this was ever the case in South Carolina my memory furnishes me with no instances of it. I have every reason to believe the contrary, having known instances of indigo planters who were by no means successful planters, who nevertheless acquired fortunes by the natural increase of their negroes.

Before the revolution Monck's Corner was a place of some commercial importance. There were three or four well-kept taverns, and five or six excellent stores. These were generally branches of larger establishments in Charleston, and as they sold goods at Charleston prices they commanded a fair business. The usual practice of the Santee planter was to take his crop to Monck's Corner, sell it there, receiving cash or goods in exchange, dine, and return home in the afternoon.

After indigo had become a valueless drug the planters turned their attention to the culture of rice, and brought into cultivation every branch and inland swamp which could produce it. After it was harvested it was prepared for the market by the slow and laborious process of beating by the hand. This was done with a pestle in mortars holding each three pecks of rough rice. This was an extra task, performed on some plantations before daylight, on others after nightfall. In the course of time those who had water-power constructed rice mills ; others used a machine with from four to six pestles. This was generally worked by oxen and was called the " pecker machine."

In my boyhood there was not a four-wheeled carriage owned in that part of Santee which I have been describing, with the exception of a heavy and unsightly vehicle, something like a baggage wagon, owned by General Marion. It was called a caravan and was drawn by four horses, ridden by postilions. The vehicle in common use was the chair. It was strongly built, wide, and roomy; three persons could be comfortable on the seat, and several children could sit on small benches in the bottom. Some years afterwards a few persons used a lighter description of carriage called coaches; these were very much like a modern carriage cut in two. They had a seat in the back; in front was the dicky seat. When four horses were used, as was frequently the case, the leaders were managed by a postilion mounted on the near horse. About the year 1800 carriages became more common. Without being more commodious than those now in use, they were very costly and heavy. Every panel had a glass and venetian blinds; they generally cost a thousand dollars, and required to be drawn by four horses.

Few horses were then furnished from the West. The planters generally raised as many as they wanted. In the inventory of the property of Peter Sinkler destroyed by the British, mentioned in another part of this paper, are more than forty brood animals.

Until the establishment of manufactories in this country all articles of furniture, clothing, etc., were dear. A good hat cost from ten to twelve dollars; a pair of boots from twelve to fifteen dollars; a dress coat from forty to sixty dollars; and other articles in proportion. Our mothers had to pay five or six shillings a yard for stuff not neater, nor prettier, nor perhaps not superior to that which may now be had everywhere for one eighth of a dollar.

Before the revolution and some time afterwards the people of St. Stephen's enjoyed a greater share of health than they have since experienced. A few facts will establish this. Whilst this portion of the State was held by the British, military posts were established at Fairlawn, Monck's Corner, Lifeland, and other places, some on the very edge of the swamp, and others on spots which have subsequently been found to be equally unhealthful. The garrisons of these posts, consisting of English, Scotch, Irish, and German troops, all enjoyed a reasonable degree of health. Three or four weeks before the battle of Eutaw, three regiments of Irish troops, just landed in Charleston, were marched into the country and were engaged in that battle. These facts are derived not from our fathers alone, who knew the truth, but from Dr. Jackson, author of the " Diseases of Tropical Climates," who was in that army. It was then a common practice with some families in Charleston to choose the fruit season, *i. e.,* July and August, to visit their friends on the river, and spend weeks there without any apprehension of danger. Nay, I have been assured by those who have been actors in these scenes, that parties would come up from Charleston in midsummer to enjoy bream and trout fishing on the Santee. They would, after an early breakfast, be on the river or lake by sunrise, dine in the swamp on the fish they had caught, and spend the rest of the day in hunting deer. These hunting and fishing frolics would last about a week, and no consequences injurious to health followed.

After the year 1790, when freshets in the river became more frequent, the climate became more sickly. The residents along the swamp suffered severely from agues and fever, and it was observed with surprise, and it still remains a mystery, that overseers and negroes and others who lived entirely in the swamp enjoyed more health than those who lived on the uplands. Capt. James Sinkler, who was a sagacious observer, was led from his observations to believe that a pine-land residence, even but a short distance from the swamp, would secure its occupants from fever. Acting on this notion, he built a house for himself in the pine land, and in June, 1793, retreated to it with a family, blacks and whites included, of more than twenty persons. In November, he returned to his plantation, having passed the summer in the enjoyment of uninterrupted health. This experiment was immediately imitated. Pineville was first settled in 1794, by Capt. John Palmer, Peter Gaillard, John Cordes, Philip Porcher, Samuel Porcher, and Peter Porcher. The liability to fevers, which was a bar to the enjoyment of happiness, being thus happily prevented, a suffering people quickly became contented and happy.

No circumstance has contributed more to the welfare of the low country than the discovery of a region in which the planters could enjoy health and at the same time be near their plantations.   It has, in fact, prevented the depopulation of the country. Other advantages followed; numbers being collected together in one village, they were enabled to establish a church, a school, a library, a market, besides the countless little comforts which are within the reach only of numbers.   The country still remained under the supervision of the proprietors ; a vigilant police was established.   These villages are fortresses where they are most useful, and secure to their owners a well-governed and therefore an obedient, well-ordered, and happy body of slaves.

When the war broke out, the churches in these parishes were closed, and nearly all the clergy resigned and left the State.   They were generally royalists and Englishmen, and a portion of their salaries was paid by the "Society in London for the Propagation of the Gospel in Foreign Parts." During the war, many of the beautiful houses which had been erected for the worship of God were used by the British as store-houses, sometimes even as stables, and several, when they were forced to abandon the country, were ruthlessly set fire to and burned down.   On the return of peace, the religious sentiment of the people was found to have suffered sadly in consequence of the long deprivation of habitual public religious worship. A rigid morality took the place of the religion of the gospel, and many believed that morality was religion. The churches which had not been destroyed were subsequently reopened, and their pulpits supplied by ministers from England. But these persons were too often utterly unfit for their sacred office, some of them positively wanting even the habit of a decent morality. The people were disgusted with them, and the churches were again closed.

It is difficult to estimate the injury done to the cause of religion by these unworthy ministers. It may give you some idea of the state of destitution of this prosperous district, when I tell you that in 1786 I was baptized by a minister who lived more than fifty miles off, and whose presence among us was accidental, and that I never again saw a minister until I was twelve years of age, and of course had never entered a house of worship. The church was not permanently reopened in St. Stephen's Parish until 1812.

During this barren and mournful period, there lived in the midst of us a man of God. He was poor in the wealth of the world ; but in love, in faith in his Redeemer, and in the works which characterize a true disciple, he stood in the front rank of all the men it has ever been my fortune to know. He was a remembrancer to those about him of the reality of God's existence, as the proper object of our af-

fection and our worship.   Often when a boy have I
seen him on a little pony riding through our plantation on his way to church in Christ Church Parish.
forty miles distant ; and when I heard him reply to
my father, who asked him the object of his journey,
that there was to be sacrament in Mr. McCauley's
church, I could scarcely take my eyes from him ; not
because I admired his zeal or his fidelity, but because
I thought he must be a fool.   Mr. McCauley was a
Presbyterian and a man of some note in his day.

In my frequent rambles amid these now deserted
plantations, I often stop to gaze on the ruins which
present themselves to my view.   I feel lost in painful wonder at the utter desolation of these places :
not a living soul is there ; not a living thing that I
can see.   Not a sigh, not a whisper, not a sound of
life comes from these ruins.   The silence of death is
everywhere.   Not even the wail of a bird of prey
reaches me through these shattered walls.   There
is nothing but ruin everywhere.   Not a bird of
good or evil omen sits upon these fragments.   Not
a wild beast haunts these ruins.   All is still, and
silent, and lifeless. I sit upon a fallen tree or a heap
of broken bricks, and look with a saddened heart
upon this scene of desolation ; and I wonder what
has become of all who once lived here—the good,

the wicked, the beautiful, the gay. How lived they; how died they? Are all their deeds buried with them? and is nothing left but the brief record of others? Was happiness within these walls? Did those who dwelt within them feel as we do, who now look upon these ruins? Did they too look back upon the past and forward to the future, and then turn to dust at last, feed the worms of the earth, and nourish the weeds that cover it? Are these masses of ruins all that they have left to bear witness of their lives? In the graveyard, the resting-place of the dead, there is only the gloom of death. Silence is becoming there; it is what we naturally expect. But here, in the abiding-place of men, where was once the din of busy life, we have now the silence of death, and more than its gloom. For these walls were meant for the living, but now no living soul dwells within them.

SAMUEL DUBOSE.

HISTORICAL AND SOCIAL SKETCH

OF

CRAVEN COUNTY, SOUTH CAROLINA.

BY FREDERICK A. PORCHER, ESQ.

[From the April, 1852, No. of *Southern Quarterly Review.*]

HISTORICAL AND SOCIAL SKETCH.

This *brochure* from the Charleston press[1] constitutes a sufficient text for us, while we seek to report the domestic and social history, from the earliest known periods of the region of country in which the scene is laid. Our beginning is fairly made by Oldmixon in his " Carolina." " We come now," saith this old chronicler, "to South Carolina, which is parted from North by Zantee River. The adjacent county is called Craven County; it is pretty well inhabited by English and French ; of the latter there is a settlement on Zantee River, and they were very instrumental in the irregular election of the Unsteady Assembly. . . . This county sends ten members to the Assembly." This is all from him, but it is enough. "The Unsteady Assembly" is, itself, a text. We shall expatiate on what he has so briefly said, and to add to the extent of the history, if we do not greatly increase its value. Our work is not that of the review exactly ; but there is noth-

[1] " The Golden Christmas : a Chronicle of St. John's Berkeley." Compiled from the Notes of a Briefless Barrister. By the author of " The Yemassee," " Guy Rivers," " Katharine Walton," etc. Charleston : Walker, Richards, & Co., 1852.

ing misplaced in subjecting countries to the same
treatment which we bestow on books.   It is as an
old resident that we give our regards to Craven
County in South Carolina.

Local attachments are strongest among the inhabitants of the country.   Those especially whose
youth has been nurtured among mountains, are
bound by a chain stronger than adamant to the
homes of their infancy.   The denizen of a crowded
metropolis is vain-glorious, perhaps proud, of his
city, but he has no love for it.   He forms a very in-
significant atom in the vast mass of humanity which
surrounds him, and he easily transfers his affection
to whatsoever portion of the world may contain his
household gods.   Not so with the rural citizen or
the inhabitant of a village.   No throng of uninter-
ested spectators ever torments him with a consciousness of his own littleness.   He feels that he is a man
of note ; that he holds a conspicuous and an important place in society ; he can calculate the political
value of his life.   He doubts whether his existence
is not necessary to the well-being of the world ; and
he rewards, with the devotion of his whole heart, the
spot which confers such importance upon him.

It has been remarked, in many localities, that the
youth who had grown up amid them, however far
they may have roamed in quest of fortune, invariably
return to close their days within reach of the scenes
hallowed by their early associations.   It is said that

every sweep who ascends the chimneys of Paris, has constantly in his mind the picture of some cherished nook in the Savoy Alps, the hope of returning to which, as its owner, gives him courage to toil and fortitude to save the rewards of his labors. Think not, as you view the uninteresting faces of these apparently hapless children of poverty, that all is dark and desolate within their bosoms. They are animated with a hope which many a more fortunate-looking man might envy. Their hearts retain vividly the impressions of happiness once enjoyed, and beat with exultation as each hour of toil brightens the prospect of resuming it. What to them are the tall and gloomy chimneys of the gay metropolis? They are the portals through which they approach their Alpine farms. But alas! well has the old French romancer sung :

> " Oh ne le quittez pas ; c'est moi qui vous le dis
> Le devant de la porte où l'on jouait jadis ;
> L'église où tout enfant, d'une voix douce et claire,
> Vous chantiez à la messe auprès de votre mère ;
> Et la petite école, où trainant chaque pas,
> Vous alliez le matin—oh ne la quittez pas."

He who would be happy amid the scenes of his infancy must so live as to preserve the freshness of that age. Time and absence efface nearly all that was hallowed to the youthful mind, and too frequently the success of the young adventurer, instead of leading him to the realization of his happiness, only awakens him from the enjoyment of a delicious day-dream.

Next to mountains, the forest possesses an irresistible charm for the imagination. Its sublime loneliness is relieved by the endless changes which the seasons, in their order, bring forth, and each, in its turn, affects the mind of the beholder. There is an indescribable charm in a northern forest when the earth is covered with snow, and the bare trees stand as if mourning over the desolation which has overtaken them. But the sweetest sensations are those excited by the pine forests of our southern soil. Here nature dies not, but only takes her rest. Her trees, which give character to the scene, are always verdant, but their verdure has none of the witchery of a more genial season. The tall and branchless monarchs of the forest rear their heads aloft to meet the rays of the sun, and as they catch the chilling blast which salutes them, utter a low and melancholy murmur of complaint as they bow before the mysterious breeze. Nor is the prospect enlivened by the sight of animal life. The solitary woodpecker mingles no melody with the tapping of his bill as he industriously pursues his food. The hoarse croaking of the crow is in perfect harmony with the scene. The gray squirrel regards, partly with astonishment, partly with alarm, the disturber of his quiet home. The whole scene is the abode of solitude, but not that which depresses the heart.

" To sit on rocks, to muse o'er flood and fell,
   To slowly trace the forest's shady scene,
   Where things that own not man's dominion dwell,
   And mortal foot hath ne'er or rarely been ;
   To climb the trackless mountain all unseen,
   With the wild flocks that never need a fold ;
   Alone o'er steeps and foaming falls to lean.
   This is not solitude ; 't is but to hold
   Converse with nature's charms, and view her charms unroll'd."

That portion of Craven County which lies south
of Santee River is marked by this species of solitary
grandeur, heightened, however, by an association
with former animation. He who travels in winter
from the bank of the Santee Canal towards the
east will find himself in an almost uninterrupted
forest of pines. On his left lie the mysterious
depths of the Santee Swamp, whose soil, once teem-
ing with the rewards of industry, is now abandoned
to the hand of nature ; before and around him the
tall pines, with their melancholy moan, spread themselves in an apparently impenetrable mass. Here
and there a broad and well-worn avenue leading
from the wood, or a stately time-honored mansion,
seen in the distance, heightens the sense of solitari-
ness by suggesting ideas of society. As you proceed, you find yourself in the streets of a village ;
but the houses are built with a special reference to
the preservation of the trees ; and the closed doors
and windows of these dwellings, their chimneys,
from which issues no hospitable smoke, recall vividly

to the imagination the idea of a city of the dead.
But the neat church, with its modest belfry, suggests
the idea of a Christian life ; while, on clearing the
skirts of the village, a well-beaten track, with all the
appointments of a race-course, indicates that this
eminently southern sport has its votaries. The road
now leaves all vestiges of life, but it is good, and
there is a something about it, its firm and well-
beaten track nearly overgrown with turf, contrasting
curiously with the neglected ditches which define its
limits on either side, that mysteriously recalls the
notion of ancient grandeur. Now it crosses one of
the great highways to the metropolis ; and now appears a low wooden building, containing one apartment, with a table extending nearly its whole length,
and benches on either side. This is the club-house,
where the citizens meet from time to time for
the unrestrained enjoyment of social and convivial
intercourse. At every step as you proceed you find
traces of former industry. Large circular tumuli
abound, bearing on their surface trees of venerable
age, which have grown up since the mounds were
formed in the process of making tar. And now,
too, you see the trunks of trees, with their barks
neatly and carefully stripped to a great height, pre-
senting to a lively imagination the appearance of an
innumerable assemblage of tombstones. These are
the marks of the turpentine gatherers, and this display of the presence of recent activity heightens the

impression of the solitude which actually surrounds you.

While the mind is thus carried from one depth of loneliness to another, a dull object appears indistinctly before you ; as you approach, its form gradually reveals itself, and soon the old parish church of St. Stephen stands before you—a handsome brick edifice. It stands at the head of one road which comes from the south, and is so situated that it may be seen at a considerable distance by those who approach it, either from the east or the west, by the main or river road. The church tells a story of former grandeur and of present desolation ; though not large, it indicates a respectable congregation ; it is finished with neatness, with some pretensions even to elegance, and the beholder involuntarily mourns over the ruin to which it is doomed.[1] All around it are graves ; these seem to be literally running into the woods ; some are marked by stones, which record the virtues of those whose remains now form part of the soil ; some, set apart for families, are enclosed by walls of brick or of perishable timber, and many are protected from the ravages of obtrusive cattle by logs rudely piled

---

[1] Since this has been written, the public spirit of some of the citizens of Pineville and its vicinity has repaired the church, and divine service is occasionally performed there. It is, however, doomed to ruin. Situated beyond the convenient reach of the people, it is maintained only by a feeling of reverence for the past. It is not hazarding much to predict that this will not suffice to preserve it for any considerable period.

around the humble mound which covers the deceased. Of the monuments to the dead, some are in perfect harmony with the church; the stones have fallen from their places, and the eye with difficulty deciphers the names of those who have long ceased to be numbered among the inhabitants of earth. Others have all the brightness which indicates that they have just left the hands of the sculptor, and here and there a melancholy mound is seen, whose freshness shows that time has not yet allowed this last memorial to be offered to departed worth. Here, then, lie the dead of Craven County —here lie those whose taste planned, and whose energy reared, this elegant temple; and here, too, lie those who but yesterday gazed like us upon this strange scene, and experienced the same emotions which now overpower our minds. Here, all is past. To them the present is an impossibility. The father and the son, the old and the young, the long forgotten, and the recently loved, all lie here together in one common past, and link it strangely and fearfully with the future!

Before such a scene what vague and undefined thoughts flit across the mind! If you stand on the north side of the church and look through the open doors (and they are never closed), you see a road coming from the south, whose well-beaten track the eye can distinguish until the sense of sight is overpowered by the distance. On the right and on the

left the same dull, unbroken line of road is seen—
their well-defined track is all that breaks the monotony of the forest ; and they, perhaps, even add to
its impressiveness by opening a vista through which
its extent may be more sensibly felt. Strange and
mysterious traces of life and of civilization ! To
what end do they appear to have been constructed ?
In this perfect solitude, whence do they come ?
Whither do they lead ? Strange, that in this spot
they should unite ! that they all lead to the grave !
that one of them must have been the last over
which these innumerable slumberers must have
been respectively borne !

That portion of Craven County which lies south
of the Santee River comprises the parishes of St.
James, Santee, and St. Stephen. Its extent to the
north of the Santee appears never to have been de-
fined. Near the line which now divides these two
parishes stood the village of Jamestown, remarkable
as being one of the principal settlements of the
French Huguenots. In 1704 the Church of England was, by act of Assembly, established in South
Carolina, and two years afterwards the French of
this town were, on their own petition, erected into a
parish and indulged with a ritual in their own lan-
guage. The whole of that long and narrow tract of
land, which extends from the canal into the sea
(about fifty miles), and lies between the river and
those parishes which constituted Berkeley County,

was known as Santee Parish, which, as it became settled, was distinguished into English and French Santee, from the character of its inhabitants ; the former occupying the part since built by the descendants of the latter, and known as St. Stephen's Parish. The French emigrants were attracted to three principal points out of Charleston ; these were : the head-waters of Ashley River, Wassamassaw ; that large feeder of Cooper River, known as French Quarter Creek ; and Jamestown.

Lawson, who visited the Santee in 1700, found about fifty French families settled on its banks; but he does not appear to have known of the existence of Jamestown. These Frenchmen, he says, generally follow a trade with the Indians, for which they are conveniently situated. His brief notice of these people proves that they made a very favorable impression upon him. In one passage he says :

"Meeting with several creeks, the French, whom we met coming from their church, were very officious in assisting with their small dories to pass over these waters ; they were all clean and decent in their apparel, their houses and plantations suitable in neatness and contrivance. They are all of the same opinion with the church of Geneva, there being no difference among them concerning the punctilios of their Christian faith ; which union hath propagated a happy and delightful concord in all other matters throughout the whole neighborhood ; living amongst themselves as one tribe or kindred, every one making it his business to be assistant to the wants of his countrymen, preserving his estate and reputation with the same exactness and concern as he does his own ; all seeming to share in the misfortunes, and rejoice in the advance and rise of their brethren."

Of these Frenchmen, who were destined to affect so powerfully the social condition of lower Carolina, it were to be wished that our traveller had given some particulars in addition to the above. He mentions having stopped at four houses : those of Mr. Huger, the ancestor of the numerous family of that name ; of Mr. Gaillard, sen., and Mr. Gaillard, jr., and of Mr. Gendron.

The name of this last gentleman is extinct, but his blood flows in the veins of a numerous posterity. We, long ago, found a copy of his will, by which it appears that he had a son and five daughters. These married, respectively, Mr. Cordes, Mr. Porcher, Mr. Huger, and Mr. Prioleau. To each of them he bequeaths a sum of money and some articles of housekeeping, particularly feather-beds. To a fifth daughter, who was yet unmarried (qui reste à marier) he leaves a double portion. Tradition has married her to a Mr. Douxsaint, without posterity. His son, John, was his residuary legatee ; and to him he leaves his coopers' tools, his slaves, both negroes and Indians, and, among other enumerated articles, his swivels or cannons. Why a private citizen should be in possession of swivels is not very easily explained. It has been suggested that about the year 1704, when the colony was at war with the authorities at St. Augustine, the danger of a piratical Spanish invasion might have induced all the substantial citizens on the rivers to provide themselves with these arms. The first page of Mr. Gendron's will is the confession of faith of a humble and grateful Christian ; and his attachment to his church is exhibited by a moderate legacy to the churches of Jamestown and Charleston, which, he says, "they shall continue to enjoy so long as they are reformed as they are at present."

This respectable emigrant has not obtained a name in history, but the traditions of Craven County still preserve it in connection with a little incident which, in the hands of Sterne, might have served as the groundwork of an immortal work. Business having carried Mr. Gendron to Charleston, his absence was so long and so unaccountably protracted that his friends supposed him to have been lost. On Sunday, while assembled at their house of worship in Jamestown, the preacher from his pulpit saw approaching up the river the canoe of his long-lost friend. Forgetting, in his joy, the sermon which he had prepared, with the exclamation, "Voila, Mr. Gendron !" he announced his safe arrival, and rushed out, followed by the delighted congregation, to welcome him whom they had mourned as dead.

Mr. John Gendron, the son of this gentleman, is mentioned by Capt. Palmer, in the Appendix to

Ramsay's South Carolina, as the commander of a company of Charleston militia in the war against the Yemassees in 1715. Though never holding a commission higher than that of a colonel, yet, from being a very long time the senior colonel in the province, he was, by courtesy, invested with the title and dignity of a brigadier. His daughter married Mr. John Palmer, the father of the author of the article just referred to, and with him the name became extinct in South Carolina.

The French emigrants to this province appear to have been governed by a principle of common-sense which reflects infinite credit on their character. They regarded Carolina as their home. Having placed themselves under the protection of the British crown, they resolved to conduct themselves like faithful subjects. Hence no attempt was made to perpetuate the remembrance of a distinct nationality. Their children were not encouraged to speak French ; and the great charity which they founded bears the name, not of a sect, nor of a foreign nation, but the catholic name of that colony which they had adopted as their native land.[1] Still, however, in their domestic life traces of their origin may be discovered. The pillau is a common dish upon their tables, and I believe that in every Huguenot house on Santee that cake which the

[1] The South Carolina Society ; which arose from the Two-Bit Club, A. D. 1737.

English know as the waffle is called the gauffre.
In summer the superfluous fresh beef is still *jerked*
for keeping, and potted beef and venison still continue to delight the senses of the people with their
grateful savor.   We are uncertain whether the
general preference of coffee over tea is the result of
an hereditary national taste, or whether it originated
in the superior cheapness of the former article.
Names still preserve their old pronunciations in
that region, and in spite of the refinements and im-
provements of modern society, the Duboses and
Marions are pertinaciously called Debusk and
Mâhrion.

Of the public life of those worthy emigrants who
found a home on the banks of the Santee, few, if
any, traces are to be found in our histories.
The English portion of the population appear to
have viewed them with feelings of hostility.   In the
disturbances which occurred during the turbulent
administration of Gov. Moor, they are represented
as having yielded too readily to the wishes of the
constituted authorities, and to have aided materially
in returning to the Assembly members who were
disposed to second and forward the ambitious views
of the governor.   During the administration of Sir
Nathaniel Johnston, who succeeded Gov. Moor, Mr.
John Ash was sent by the English Dissenters to
plead their cause against the usurpation of the High
Church party.   In his representation of the affairs

of the colony, he says : " That at the election for Berkley and Craven counties the violence of Mr. Moor's time, and all other illegal practices, were with more violence repeated, and openly avowed by the present governor and his friends : Jews, strangers, sailors, servants, negroes, and almost every Frenchman in Craven and Berkley counties came down to elect, and their votes were taken, and the persons by them voted for were returned by the sheriffs." At this time it appears that Charleston was the only place in the colony at which polls were opened, and here it was necessary for citizens from every county to come, in order to enjoy the elective franchise.[1] The Assembly they elected established

---

[1] Such appears to have been the custom. Mr. F. Yonge, in his account of the revolutionary proceedings in 1719, declares it to have been so. The subject, however, is not very clear. In the first place, it would have been difficult, in a town devoted to the dissenting interest, for the concourse of voters from Colleton and Craven counties to create such disturbances as Oldmixon describes ; and, secondly, the act of Assembly of 1804, for better ordering elections, clearly intimates, though it does not direct, that a poll should be opened in each county. It provides—1st. That no votes be taken by proxy ; 2d. That if the sheriffs neglect to hold a poll in a county, the people may vote in the adjoining one ; and 3d. That the polls shall be held in an open and public place. But those counties had not at that time any court-house, and Mr. Yonge declares that the whole House of Assembly was chosen in Charleston until the administration of Gov. Daniel (1718), when it was enacted that every parish shall send a certain number of delegates (36 in all), who shall be balloted for at their respective churches, or other convenient place, by virtue of writs directed to the church-wardens, who were to make a return of the persons elected. It was the veto upon this act by Gov. Johnson, at the suggestion of Mr. Rhett and Chief-Justice Trott, which was one of the leading causes of the revolution of 1719, which shook off the Proprietary government.

the Church of England in the colony, but with such provisions that the Bishop of London and the Society for Propagating the Gospel in America resolved not to send or support any missionaries in the province until the act, or the clause relating to the establishment of lay commissioners, should be annulled.

Oldmixon says that the law was declared null and void by Queen Anne, at the suggestion of the House of Lords; but, as the act still remains on the statute-book, and the church continued from that date (1704) to receive the aid of the state, as well as of the Society for Propagating the Gospel, it is more likely that the offensive clauses were rendered inoperative, without being formally annulled. The act of conformity was passed by a vote of twelve members against eleven dissentients. A full house numbered thirty members, so that this act was passed by little more than a third of the whole house. Every Dissenter was thereupon turned out of his seat, and his place supplied by the person, being a Churchman, who had the most votes next to him. In six months afterwards, the same Assembly, in a full house, passed a bill to repeal the act, but it was rejected in the upper house, and the governor, in great indignation, dissolved the Commons' house, by the name of the Unsteady Assembly.

During this period of the colonial existence, the only part of Craven County which was settled was

that portion now known as St. James' Santee, and
soon afterwards, called French Santee, to distinguish
it from what was afterwards St. Stephen's Parish,
or, as it was formerly called, English Santee. The
legal separation of the two parishes was effected in
1754, and the brick church, which we have noticed
in the early part of this essay, was commenced in
1762.

It has not been the lot of this section of the
country to produce many persons whose names have
filled a niche in the temple of fame. The virtues
of its citizens have been of a character more domestic than those which generally receive the chaplet of
immortality. Engaged in the quiet and all-absorb-
ing pursuits of agriculture, they cared not to stir in
the bustling world of politics, and as a proof of the
contented spirit of the people it may be remarked
that in the war of the revolution a large number ad-
hered to the king.

Agriculture and Indian trade were the occupations of the early French settlers. The latter
source of profit was extinguished by the gradual
settlement of the country ; the former continued to
give wealth to its votaries. The French, from the
quarter of Wassamassaw, gradually left their seats
and settled on the fertile bank of the Santee, and by
the commencement of the revolution, English Santee, or St. Stephen, had passed almost entirely into
their hands.

Among the French, an individual, whose name has not transpired, adopted a pursuit which many will suppose characteristic. "A French dancing-master," says Oldmixon, "settling in Craven County, taught the Indians country dances, to play on the flute and the hautboy, and got a good estate, for it seems the barbarians encouraged him with the same extravagance as we do the dancers, singers, and fiddlers of his countrymen."

One citizen of this parish has earned for himself a name in the world of letters, and it is strange that Ramsay, who appears to have sought eagerly after Carolinian celebrities, should have entirely ignored his existence.   Thomas Walter, an English gentleman whose devotion to the cause of science led him to the wilds of Carolina, was attracted by the charms of Miss Peyre, of St. Stephen, married her, and settled there.   He devoted himself particularly to the pursuit of botany, and the curious are still occasionally rewarded by a visit to his garden, the ruins of which may still be seen near the banks of the Santee Canal.   He is the ancestor of one branch of the Porcher family, and of the Charlton family of Georgia.   His book, the " Flora Caroliniana, which was printed in London in 1789, is dated ad Ripas Fluvii Santee.

Walter was married a short time before the battle of Black Mingo.   Among the loyalist officers who were defeated on that occasion was Mr. John Peyre, the brother of Mrs. Walter. Marion's patience had been sorely tried by the pertinacity with which these gentlemen maintained the conflict, and for this reason, and perhaps as a sort of retaliatory measure, for the unjustifiable deportation of the Charleston prisoners to St. Augustine, he vowed a terrible revenge against any who might hereafter fall into his hands. It was Mr. Peyre's fate to be captured and to experience this revenge. He was allowed none of the privileges awarded to prisoners of war, but was sent to Philadelphia for safe keeping, and there, for several months, dragged out a miserable existence in a loathsome dungeon; when at length released, he was unceremoniously turned into the street, almost naked and altogether miserable. In his distress he accosted a Quaker in the street, whose benevolent face attracted him. The Quaker heard his story, and taking fifty dollars from his pocket, gave them to him, advising him to procure decent clothing and go home. Mr. Peyre earnestly entreated that he might learn the name of his generous benefactor, in order that, when in his power, he might discharge the obligation, but the old man refused. " Consider this money," said he, " as a loan, and you will sufficiently discharge it by giving to any one whom you shall find in circumstances of similar distress."

The name of Peyre, once an honored and a flourishing name in this parish, is now extinct.

The last who bore it was Thomas Walter Peyre, grandson of the botanist, a gentleman whom none knew but to love, honor, and esteem. Modest and retiring, even to a fault, he was, in all other respects, a perfect model of a useful country gentleman. His home was the abode of religion, order, skill, economy, and enlightened liberality. His friends were devoted, and the rectitude of his principles and the general amiability of his conduct gained him the good-will and respect of all. His death has caused a chasm in his circle which will not be filled whilst the freshly turned turf continues to announce the recentness of his decease ; and as he never married, the name of Peyre was buried in his grave.

Though the body of Marion reposes in a grave in St. Stephen's Parish, Craven County cannot number him among her notabilities. Both Georgetown and St. John's Berkeley claim the honor of his birth. The latter was, unquestionably, the place of his residence.

But the widow of General Marion certainly did live and die in St. Stephen's Parish ; and there also lived a large number of his friends, relations, and companions in arms. There, especially, was his memory revered ; and there, to this day, you will hear but one opinion expressed respecting the merits of Weems' life of Marion—that of unmitigated disgust.

We have not the smallest disposition to detract from the merit of General Marion. We have a child's recollection of his widow ; we never knew her but as my grandmamma, for so she insisted upon being called by every child ; and we have been taught to believe, as an article of religion, that her husband was vilely treated by his reverend biographer. We have seen this book circulating in every part of the United States, and were always ready, to the expressions of admiration with which its perusal is everywhere else greeted, to reply, with the scornful sneer of superior knowledge, that Marion's friends rejected the book as a libel on his fair fame. The indignation with which the book was received is hardly yet appeased. The offended widow loudly declared that she would willingly, if in her power, punish the transgressor with stripes ; and numerous friends sympathized with her outraged feelings. But now that nearly fifty years have passed, what is the true estimate to be placed upon the book? Next to Washington, what general of revolutionary memory has so wide a fame? From the Hudson to the extremity of the Far West, from Florida to the Falls of St. Anthony, his name is perpetuated in towns, counties, and colleges. And what is the cause of this unusual popularity? Surely not the brief notices of his exploits in any general history of the war. Surely not the extensive circulation of his biography by Judge James.[1] No ; it is the

---

[1] We do not mention Simms' Biography, because that, having been executed within a few years, has had, and could have had, no influence in producing this effect.

irresistible influence of Weems' book—a work whose popularity daily increases, and which is destined to transmit to posterity, in colors ever brightening, the memory of the active and clever leader of the undaunted Whigs of Carolina. Peaceful be the repose of the venerable lady and her generous allies ; they owe to their supposed calumniator a debt of gratitude. For so long as Marion's name shall be honored, prosperity will reverence the virtuous lady who blessed him with her love.

It is well known that General Marion never had a child. With that instinctive desire of living in posterity which clings to us and becomes more urgent as we advance towards the termination of our career, he adopted a nephew who assumed his name. But, by a singular fatality, this gentleman, who was twice married, and had eleven daughters, never had the happiness to see a son. Two young men, great-nephews of the General, are all who are left to perpetuate this ancient Huguenot name. It is to be hoped that they will be mindful of the sacred duty committed to them, and faithfully discharge it.

The most eminent military character which the revolution produced, in this parish, was Col. Hezekiah Maham. Like the respected names of Gendron and Peyre, this, too, has become extinct. Maham was a colonel of cavalry in the revolutionary war, and was distinguished not only for his gallantry, but also for a certain skill in the art of reducing fortified places. It was at his suggestion that the expedient was first adopted (similar, by the way, to the method practised in the middle ages) of constructing against such places a tower of logs so high as to command them. This was first practised at Fort Watson, and the description of Weems, which I give, is all that can be wished. " Finding that the fort mounted no artillery, Marion resolved to make his approaches in a way that should give his riflemen a fair chance against the musqueteers. For this purpose large quantities of pine logs were cut, and, as soon as dark came on, were carried in perfect silence within point-blank shot of the fort, and run up in the shape of large pens or chimney stacks considerably higher than the enemy's parapets. Great, no doubt, was the consternation of the garrison next morning, to see themselves thus suddenly overlooked by this strange kind of steeple, pouring down upon them from its blazing tops incessant showers of rifle bullets. . . . Our riflemen lying above them, and firing through loopholes, were seldom hurt ; while the British, obliged every time they fired, to show their heads, were frequently killed." Weems, who does not once mention Maham's name in his book, ascribes the invention solely to Marion. Lee, on the contrary, gives Maham credit both for the design and the execution ; and he frequently, afterwards, speaks of

the Maham tower, as an efficient and decisive
means of reducing the simple forts of the interior.

Not the least evil attendant upon civil war is,
that notions of right and wrong become so con-
founded in our minds, that we are more disposed
to reconcile morality with practice, than practise
morality.   They who see acts of aggression and
violence practised with applause, are apt to forget
that they are commendable only under the severe
law of necessity, and that under other circumstances
they are rightly considered as crimes.   Men, whose
opinions are entitled to respect, have not hesitated
to ascribe the public crimes, which not long since
afflicted England, to the violences which the circumstances of civil war justified or excused ; so that
many a marauder and highwayman only continued
as a crime that course of life which he had been encouraged to commence as a duty.

These consecutive evils of civil war were felt in
Carolina.   After the revolution, the highways were
unsafe.   Many now living recollect that persons
rarely ventured to travel the Goose Creek road
without arms ; and the public execution of a man
and his wife, in Charleston, for highway robbery, as
late as 1820, bear fearful testimony to the insecurity
of life and property, even in the neighborhood of
the metropolis.

Besides highway robbery, horse-stealing was a
common crime.   Many engaged in it ; but two in-

dividuals, by name Roberts and Brown, organized it and conducted it as a matter of business. One, or both, of these men was hanged in Charleston, in 1789. They had their agents and depots arranged and organized ; and from the Santee to the wilds of Florida, they and their confederates were at once the nuisance and the terror of the country.

Mr. Thomas Palmer lived on his plantation on Fair Forest Swamp. Like other planters of the times, he possessed a large and valuable collection of horses, one of which, called Fantail, was an especial favorite. Early one morning he discovered that his stables had been opened in the night, and his best horses stolen. The alarm was quickly spread, and in a few hours a party of gentlemen set off, under the lead of Col. Maham, in pursuit of the stolen property. It was difficult to track the fugitives, but as suspicion naturally rested on Roberts and his gang, they directed their course towards Orangeburg, which was one of his head-quarters. After travelling a few miles, they met Mr. René Ravenel, who, being informed of the object of their search, informed them that, having been out early that morning, he had seen a horse, about a quarter of a mile off, crossing the road ; that a momentary glance at the hinder part of the animal, which was all that he saw, convinced him that it was Mr. Palmer's horse. The circumstance would have passed from his memory but for this meeting. He conducted the party to the spot ; numerous tracks were found, and the party, now confirmed in their suspicions, continued with renewed alacrity, determined to make a certain house in Dean Swamp the first object of their visit.

A short time before nightfall they approached the house, and determined to remain concealed until the night should be well advanced. A horse was heard to neigh ; several answered, and Mr. Palmer, turning to Col. Maham, said : " Uncle Maham, I 'll pledge my life that that is the voice of Fantail." A countryman happening to pass was detained as a prisoner. He acknowledged that he was bound to the house which the party intended to visit, and acquainted them that a large gathering of men and women was expected there that night for a frolic. With this information they were sure of their game ; and, having divided themselves into a convenient number of parties, they separated, appointing to approach the house on a certain signal, which would be given by Col. Maham. Every thing succeeded. When the noise within indicated that the frolic was going on fast and furious, the signal was given ; the parties simultaneously entered the house, and the marauders found themselves suddenly affronted by armed guests, whose presence boded them no good. They fled. The women, on the contrary, fought boldly ; and Col. Maham declared that if they had been seconded by their gallants the pursuing party would have been defeated. Aided by the courageous defence of the ladies, most of the marauders escaped ; the captured were summarily disposed of ; each was tied to a tree and flogged. The party then, recovering their stolen horses, returned homewards, leaving their prisoners, each at his tree, to be relieved when their friends should have sufficient courage to go to their assistance.

Whatever may have been Col. Maham's reputation as a soldier, it appears that he had rather crude notions of the duties of a citizen. He became indebted, and his creditor was importunate. Recourse was had to legal process, and a sheriff's officer proceeded to serve him with a writ.

One morning, just as the colonel was about to sit down to his breakfast, a stranger was announced. He went out to give him a hospitable greeting, and was instantly served with a writ. The old Whig surveyed the document with feelings of astonishment and indignation. That he, who had perilled his life and fortune in defence of his country's liberties, should be thus bearded in his own castle, and threatened with the loss of his own, was a thought not to be borne, and he instantly determined to make the unfortunate instrument of his creditor the victim. He returned the parchment to the officer with an order (and the colonel never gave a vain order) that he should instantly swallow it, and when the dry meal was fairly engulphed, he brought the man into the house and gave him good liquor to wash it down.

But the colonel discovered, like too many others who had borne the burden and heat of the day, that the civil power was in the ascendant, and that writs are not to be served up as a morning's meal. He fled the country, and remained an exile until the difficulty was removed by the intervention of his friends. He died as he had lived, on his plantation on Santee Swamp, and was buried there. His house was destroyed by fire many years since ; but we remember to have seen its chimneys standing. Within a few years a massive marble monument, visible from the road, has been erected over his grave by his descendant, Lieut. Gov. Ward.

Until the year 1794, the citizens of this parish, like those of every other part of the State, lived always on their plantations throughout the year. Some of the more wealthy had town residences to which they resorted, partly for health, but chiefly for the convenience of educating their children.

The period between the close of the war and 1794 was full of disaster to the agriculturist. The bounty on indigo, which, under the fostering care of Great Britain, had rendered that plant the staple of South Carolina, having been of course withdrawn, indigo became thenceforth an unprofitable culture. The Santee Swamp, which appeared at one time to be an inexhaustible source of wealth, had become, from the frequency, the greatness, and the irregularity of the freshets in the river, extremely precarious ; and many a planter, the amount of whose possessions would have ranked him among the wealthy, saw in his wealth only an increase of expense, and felt all the privations of poverty. In the year 1794 cotton was first cultivated in St. John's Parish by General Moultrie, and, in two years after, it became the staple of the country.

It had been observed that those persons who lived in the pine lands were usually exempt from those distressing autumnal intermittent fevers, which are the bane of our country, and several gentlemen determined to avail themselves of this fact for the purpose of improving the social condition of the country. Accordingly, in 1794, Capt. John Palmer, Capt. Peter Gaillard, Mr. John Cordes, Mr. Samuel Porcher, Mr. Peter Porcher, and Mr. Philip Porcher, built for themselves houses in the pine land, near to each other, and thus laid the foundation of Pineville, the oldest settlement of the kind in the southern country. The experiment proved successful, and in a few years it became the summer residence of the planters of St. Stephen's Parish, and of those of upper and middle St. John's.

Pineville is situated on a low, flat ridge, thickly covered with pines, and dotted with small ponds and savannahs. It lies two miles south of Santee Swamp, and five miles from the river. Though the

principal growth is pine, it is not what we call a
pine barren ; for the red oak and the hickory, which
flourish on a soil under which the clay lies at no
great depth, indicate a considerable degree of natural fertility. On the south, about a quarter of a
mile from the nearest house, meanders the Crawl
branch, a swampy stream which a few miles below
feeds the Santee by the name of the Horsepen
Creek ; at the same distance to the north is Mar-
gate Swamp, a huckleberry bay, without any decided
water-course, which protrudes from the Santee
Swamp. At the period of its greatest prosperity the
village contained about sixty substantial and well-
built houses, each situated in a lot of from one to
two acres in area. The pine trees were religiously
preserved, not only within the lots, but without.
Those which were uninclosed, being the property
of the public, were protected by a fine of five dollars
imposed on any person who should cut down or by
any wanton injury threaten the life of a tree.

An opinion generally prevails that the village lost
its healthfulness in consequence of the violation of
these regulations by the people, who cut down
their trees and cultivated gardens. Never was
opinion more erroneous. In all of the original lots,
traces of cultivation may be seen. It was not then
considered dangerous to indulge in the luxury of a
garden. Farms, too, appeared in close neighborhood to the village. On the west, Greenfield farm

might be seen from the village. Clark's farm lay between it and the Crawl; and to the southwest, the Polebridge farm of Mr. Thos. Palmer, could be seen from our father's house. But in 1834 all this had been long changed. Not a garden cheered the eye of a resident; and the corporation of the Pineville Academy had purchased all these farms, and abandoned them to the possession of the pines, for the purpose of insuring the healthfulness of the place.

Health, the primary object for which Pineville was settled, being attained, the other objects soon followed, of course. In 1805 a grammar-school was established and chartered under the name of the Pineville Academy, and commenced a prosperous career under the administration of Mr. Alpheus Baker, a native of New Hampshire. Mr. Baker's reputation attracted students from various parts of the country, and his administration was, ever afterwards, regarded as a standard by which the merit of any of his successors was to be judged. He was followed, successively, by Mr. Lowry, Mr. Snowden, and Mr. Stephens, all of South Carolina; Mr. Gordon, of Maine, Mr. Gillet of Vermont, Messrs. Cain, Daniel, and Furman, of South Carolina; Messrs. Fisk, Houghton, Gere, and Leland, of Massachusetts. On the death of the last-named gentleman, in 1836, of the prevailing epidemic, all confidence in the healthfulness of the village being lost, the exercises of the school were, for several years, suspended.

Besides these gentlemen here named, others were occasionally employed as assistants, whenever the number of scholars justified the expenditure ; and, until the breaking up of the village, in 1836, the state of the school generally warranted the employment of an assistant. The principal teacher was elected by the Board of Trustees for one year. He was provided with a house, received a salary of a thousand dollars, and was required to receive a certain number of boarders at a fixed rate. These boarders were for the winter months only, as their parents were generally in the village in the summer. It would, perhaps, be invidious to notice more particularly any of these gentlemen. I shall make one exception. Mr. Yorick Sterne Gordon appeared before the trustees with credentials from the highest authority in New England. A letter from the venerable Jedediah Morse secured his election. He went to Pineville with a large collection of school-books, all of which he introduced into the academy, and on his first appearance in the school-room spoke so threateningly to the boys, that such an impression was made on their minds, that he never had occasion to resort to punishment. He exacted lessons from the boys of inordinate length, and many a tear have we shed when bedtime found us with our task not more than half accomplished. Never did man so completely subdue the spirits of a set of boys. And yet, out of school, he was sociable, and appeared disposed to promote their little pleasures; but still he was uncertain, and had we been more conversant with the world, we should have called him capricious. At a certain hour every day he was in the habit of retiring from the school-house to his dwelling, where he would spend a short time; on his return he was observed never to follow the beaten path, but to approach the school-house by zig-zag lines; and, to our simple apprehensions, this strange conduct was supposed to be directed with a view of keeping the window of the school-house always in sight, so that he could watch the boys even when he was not present. How long this fascination might have lasted I cannot say; for in less than three months after his installation, the spring holidays, for a fortnight, commenced, and, before they were over, Mr. Gordon was dead. He died of delirium tremens, and his assistant declared that he had not been sober a single day since his arrival.

The people of Pineville, would never become a corporate body. All administrative powers were, therefore, assumed by the Board of Trustees. Those being overseers of a school, they gradually became the council of a town, thus happily illustrating the insidious progress of usurpation. They acquired, either by gift or purchase, all the unoccupied lands, and as owners of the soil, made such wholesome regulations as circumstances appeared to demand.

In addition to the school, a public library was organized. This, we believe, was originated by the public spirit of Mr. Robert Marion, formerly a member of Congress from the Charleston district. The first house used for the purpose had been a chapel of ease to the parish church, about two miles to the west of the village. After the erection of the church in Pineville, this chapel became useless, and it was taken down and rebuilt in Pineville. A partition wall divided it into two rooms, whereof the inner one was set apart for the reception of books, and the outer, being a sort of ante-chamber, was used on public occasions as a town hall. In this room the patriots usually celebrated the Fourth of July, and on that day the walls, which had formerly reëchoed only to the sound of anthems and holy songs, were made to resound with the noise of revelry and uproarious patriotism. In 1826 a new library building was erected, and the old one, being sold at public auction, was purchased by a person who used the materials for the construction of a livery stable. As it is fashionable to call all libraries select, we suppose we must apply the epithet to this one also. But as we cannot find any catalogue of books which exceeds a thousand volumes, we are constrained to add that it does not appear to reflect much credit on the literary enterprise of the citizens. With the destruction of Pineville that of the library followed. The books were either lost or destroyed, and we doubt whether the shelves now contain a single volume.

The citizens of Pineville being all planters, long residents in the country, and for the most part descendants of the Huguenots of Santee Parish, were almost, as a matter of course, attached to the Episcopal Church. For several years after the foundation of the village, divine service continued to be performed in the parish church. But the course of events changed completely the condition of the parish, and by the year 1808 the church was, as it were, left in the wilderness, and the service discontinued. For a short period Mr. Baker officiated, every Sunday, as lay reader in the chapel, near the village, and it was then determined to enjoy the advantages of religious worship at home. A neat wooden church was accordingly erected in the village, and placed under the rectorship of the Rev. C. B. Snowden. Chapels for winter service, by the same rector, were soon afterwards erected in St. John's Berkeley, at Black Oak, and the Rocks, so that, though there were three different places of worship, the congregation was considered but one.

The erection of the two chapels in St. John's Berkeley gave rise to a lawsuit of a singular character, which completely destroyed the social relations existing between the upper and lower portions of that parish ; but as this is foreign to the history of Craven County, we shall not notice it here.

After a service of about ten years Mr. Snowden retired from the rectorship of the church, and was succeeded by the Rev. D. J. Campbell, who died at his post in 1840. The churches were then vacant for nearly three years, until, in 1842, they were filled by the present worthy and efficient rector, Mr. W. Dehon, who is assisted by the Rev. C. P. Gadsden.[1]

In the olden time a sermon was preached every Sunday morning. In the afternoon the congregation re-assembled, and evening prayers were read. No sermon followed ; none was expected ; I may add, none was desired.

In most country churches there is some difficulty about singing. Many, who can sing, shrink from the notoriety of assuming the functions of chorister, and very often the office is discharged by one who has no merit beyond his zeal to recommend his performance. This difficulty was generally experienced in Pineville, and the whole service was frequently performed without music. Old Capt. Palmer, the patriarch of the village, certainly possessed no musical talents, but he had zeal, and fancied that he could accomplish the hundredth psalm. This was, accordingly, the standing psalm of the morning ; and the old chorister, taking courage from his success, would, at times, boldly undertake other pieces

---

[1] Mr. Gadsden is now Assistant Rector of St. Philip's Church, Charleston.

of music. Now it is always the fate of a country chorister to be the object of envy. They who witness his success are apt to fancy they can do equally well. It so happens, therefore, that the chorister is liable to perpetual attacks, and if he is not very prompt, will find the song taken out of his mouth by these pretenders. So hath it ever been. So was it with Capt. Palmer. Others attempted to take the lead, but the indignant musician was not to be driven from his post. Sing he would ; and it was not uncommon for a whole stanza to be sung at the same time to two different tunes. In the end, however, all competition ceased, and the old gentleman reigned undisputed Director of Music.[1] It cannot be denied that, for a considerable period, our prophecy had a literal fulfilment in Pineville, for the songs of the temple were howlings. One incident occurred there lately, of so ludicrous a character that I cannot help narrating it, though it may appear inconsistent with the dignity of history. The rector was in feeble health ; he had given out a

---

[1] This difficulty appears, by an old tradition, to have been unfelt by our ancestors. Their zeal was frequently too ardent, and the delicate ear of the parson was in danger of being overpowered by strong and discordant voices. Mr. Richebourg, the pastor of Jamestown, whose attachment to Mr. Gendron was so *naïvely* exhibited, as described in our notice of Jamestown, was not blinded by his friendship into any indiscreet admiration of his voice. Thus, after announcing the hymn, he would say : " Don't sing, Mr. Gendron ; your voice is like a goat's ; you be quiet. Mr. Guerry, your voice is sweet ; you may sing." I presume Capt. Palmer inherited both the voice and the zeal of his great ancestor.

hymn to be sung before the sermon, and retired to the vestry-room to make the usual change of his vestments. The worthy chorister, who from his place could see indistinctly into the vestry-room, fancied that he saw the rector in a recumbent position, and imagined that, fatigued with the morning service, he was taking repose. Determined, therefore, to allow him ample time to rest himself, he had no sooner finished the hymn than he recommenced it, and sang it over again, to the astonishment of the whole congregation, as well as of the rector, who had entered the pulpit unperceived by his worthy friend, and was quietly waiting for the music to cease in order to begin his sermon.

About the year 1822 or 1823, a peripatetic singing-master visited Pineville, and, partly for the purpose of improvement in psalmody, partly to vary the general monotony of village life, the young people formed a class, which he instructed every alternate Saturday.

All professional singing-masters have something odd about them. Their vocation is to teach sacred music, and whether it is that they are laboring to reconcile their manners with the supposed dignity of their employment, or whether it is owing to something in the very nature of the calling which makes the profession ridiculous, we cannot determine. Certain it is, however, that from the time of David Gamut (who, by the way, was not created

when *our* singing-master flourished), down to the
itinerant professor of Tinkum, the professor of the
science of psalmody has ever been the butt of ridicule. Burbidge, the Pineville professor, was no exception; but owing to the habitual gravity of his
scholars he experienced less, perhaps, than most
others have done elsewhere. Who he was, or
whence he came, we could never learn. Regu-
larly, on every alternate Saturday, he was at his
post in the church, instructed his class, and after
partaking of the hospitality of a friendly bachelor,
who most irreverently made game of him, he appeared at church next day and comforted the heart
of the good rector by discharging, ex cathedra, the
office of chorister. This done, he disappeared, and
no more was heard of him for a fortnight. He was
a brownish man, about the middle size, with jet
black, curly, or ratherish kinky hair, very *knock-
kneed*, and his skin-tight nankeen trousers scarcely
reaching below the calf, displayed this perfection of
his figure to the greatest advantage. At that time
psalmody was always taught by means of what was
called *solmization*, or a systematic arrangement of
the syllables, *sol, la, mi, fa*, by which a tune was
sung in all of its parts without any reference to the
words ; and the great point for the learner to ascertain, in order to accomplish this, was to determine
the place of *mi*. Now we have no doubt all this
was no more intelligible to Burbidge than it is to

the greater part of our readers. To supply the deficiency of ignorant teachers, books were printed, in which these mystic syllables are indicated by the shape of the notes ; but these, of course, would never be employed by a really competent teacher. This book, however, Burbidge used. His class was arranged in three divisions, forming three sides of a square ; on the right sat the bass, in the centre the air, and the treble on the left. He stood in the centre. Then, after preluding a few notes, giving the pitch to each of the parts in succession, the music would commence, and he, with the palm of his left hand turned upwards, and that of his right downwards, would beat time, imitating the motions of a top sawyer. His class was decorous, but decorum could not always resist the strange effect of his solemn motions. We have seen *mæstri* in various opera-houses in Europe and America, and have sometimes laughed at the enthusiasm they displayed, but never did we see one more thoroughly occupied in admiration of his work than this humble *mæstro* of the village school.

Humble as he was, however, he produced fruit which was destined to be permanent. From the practice of singing in this class, confidence was acquired, and the church was no longer dumb. The humble foundation being laid, a better taste began to develop itself. But some of his tunes possessed startling merit, and in the psalmody of those churches tunes are still sung which were taught to the parents of the present generation by the obscure Burbidge.

All the objects which were hoped to result from the founding of Pineville were now accomplished. The people were blessed with health, a school flourished and placed the means of a classical education within the reach of many who would otherwise have wanted that advantage, and a church was opened every Sunday for religious worship. Let us now devote a short time to the consideration of social and domestic life in Pineville.

The inhabitants were all planters. They met without any consciousness of social inequalities, and as there were no persons either above or beneath them, their manners were distinguished by the most perfect simplicity and absence of every sort of affectation. They were all cotton planters, and had, therefore, the same interests, the same wishes, the same hopes, the same fears. In process of time, by means of intermarriage they were all connected with each other, and related by blood, so that it was a community in which the most perfect unity of sentiment and of thought prevailed. Their habits of living were as simple as their manners. It was long before any enterprising person conceived the idea of opening a market, so that the planters were supplied from the produce of their farms. On a certain day in every week a calf was killed and distributed among a club of eight persons, who united for that purpose. In the early life of the village, he who killed the calf, having for his portion the head as well as the loin, entertained all the villagers at his house and regaled them with calf's head soup. On another certain day, a lamb or a porker (called a shoat) was killed and divided among four families. Then eight or sixteen would unite for the purpose of killing and distributing a cow. Thus for three days in the week a supply of butcher's meat was furnished. The wants of the remaining days were furnished from the resources of the poultry houses of the planters. In the course of time a beef market was opened twice a week for the sale of that article. The veal, lamb, and pork were always furnished as we have described. The Santee River being near, it might have been expected that fish would frequently find its way to the table ; but the supply was meagre, and fish was always a rarity. An enterprising Yankee in the neighborhood would have made a good business by following the occupation of a fisherman. The bream of the Santee, taken from the neighborhood of Pineville, is one of the most delicious fish that is eaten.

Pineville was an isolated community. Situated about fifty miles from Charleston, in a part of the district remote from the great thoroughfares, and never frequented by wayfaring men, it was cut off from all social intercourse with people elsewhere.

When the month of June found all the villagers assembled for the summer, their feelings were somewhat analogous to those of persons who meet together on board of a ship for the purpose of making a long voyage. All commerce with the external world seemed interdicted. Entertaining an indefinable distrust of the climate of the country, they regarded their village with a sort of superstitious affection, and viewed as a calamity any accident which might make it necessary to spend a single night elsewhere. The air was not to be changed. Whether for better or for worse, he who commenced the season by breathing the air of Pineville, must continue to do so; or, if he left it, he should not return before autumn. It is not strange, therefore, that the sense of mutual dependence was intense.

And sweet and balmy is that Pineville air; inviting repose, tranquillizing the troubled frame, and filling the mind with sweet and hopeful thoughts. When the lungs, vexed and harassed by the dust of the metropolis and the cruel east winds of the coast, inhale the soft and fragrant breath of the pines, how voluptuous is the sensation of rest, of perfect repose! How great a blessing to suffering humanity has God thus deposited in the most gloomy and desolate-looking portion of his creation!

The habits of every house were alike. At sunrise breakfast was served, and the planters went out to visit their plantations. Those who owned estates in the neighborhood did this every day; others at intervals, greater or less, throughout the week. But whether he visited his plantation or not, the planter was generally on his horse, and inspected those plantations which were within an easy ride. Hunting also afforded the means of passing the time. Deer and foxes abound in the neighborhood, and the Santee Swamp would sometimes furnish a still more exciting sport by offering wolves and bears to the hunters. After the morning's ride was over, the post-office or the village store was the general rendezvous and lounging-place. Here politics and crops were the never-failing topics of conversation.

At one o'clock dinner was served. One old lady, who died in 1848, never dined later than half-past twelve. A portion of the afternoon was always devoted to sleep. Every piazza was furnished wtih long benches, and these formed the rude beds on which the gentlemen invariably indulged in the luxury of a siesta.

The siesta over, and whilst the sun was still high above the horizon, the kettle would bubble for the evening refection, and hot tea and cakes would be offered to refresh those whose heavy sleep rendered some refreshment necessary. This early meal, of course, indicated that supper would close the labors of the day. And now the active duties of the day being over, and every family having refreshed themselves with tea or coffee, social life commenced.

Every one came to tea prepared either to make or receive visits.

Bonnets and hats were articles of female dress which were entirely ignored in the Pineville evening visits. In attire a simple elegance prevailed. Young ladies usually dressed in white; the aged were clad in graver colors. Visits were unceremonious. The guests were received in the piazza. No one ever expected to be invited into the house, and persons might spend a season in social intercourse with the people, without seeing the interior of any house but their own. Sometimes chairs were offered to the visitors, but, more generally, the long benches with which the piazza was furnished were the only seats. No refreshments were offered or expected. But if any one asked for a glass of water, the experienced servant would hand a sufficient number of glasses of the pure element to satisfy every one present. For the water (got from wells) was cold, clear, insipid, and refreshing, and all seemed to sympathize in each other's thirst.

But though the visiting was done at night, and the piazza the reception room, the company did not sit in the dark. In front of the house a fire of light-wood formerly, in later times of pine-straw, was kept constantly burning. The reasons for this practice were manifold. It diffused a cheerful light over the otherwise dark and gloomy lot. The smoke, too, was supposed to be conducive to health ;

and the light certainly attracted night-flies and
moths from the inferior lights of the dwelling.
Around these fires the children would sport. Each
little fellow would take a pride in having a little
fire of his own ; the larger and more daring would
show their courage by leaping through the flames.
Around its cheerful blaze time seemed to fly on
golden wings. It was literally light to the dwelling,
and a house without its yard fire appeared desolate
and sorrow-stricken. It was the daily task of the
hostler to collect materials sufficient to keep the
light burning until bedtime. By ten o'clock social
life was over, and the repose of sleep sought.
Whilst the visitor was preparing to return home,
the servant lit his lantern, and with this simple but
necessary escort, she trod the streets of the village
with as much security as the halls of her own
mansion.

Hunting, riding, and social visiting were the
several and separate amusements of the sexes in
Pineville. The chief amusement of which they par-
took, in common, was dancing. The languid city
belle, who cannot conceive of the exertion necessary
to a dance in summer, except, indeed, under the
exhilarating influence of a watering-place, may
stare ; but the unsophisticated youth of both sexes
in Pineville regarded dancing as both proper and
natural. The month of June would be devoted to
feeling at home, and then, by way of making a

start, the Fourth of July would be celebrated by a ball. This first taste would be followed by a desire for more. During the heat of summer, parties, simple and of short duration, would be arranged by the gentlemen—a certain number, in turn, bearing the moderate expense and acting as managers, so as to have one every fortnight. At these parties the company would assemble early, and by midnight all would be quiet. As summer would wane the passion would increase. The public assemblies were found to be of too rare occurrence, and all sorts of expedients would be resorted to for the purpose of getting up a dance. If a lady should put her patchwork quilt in the quilting frame, the young ladies would go in the evening to assist in the interesting occupation of quilting, and the young gentlemen would go to assist the latter in threading their needles. The rest may easily be guessed. In a short time the quilting frame would disappear, and the young people would be found threading the mazes of the dance. Benevolent ladies, too, would be importuned, and not in vain, to throw open their rooms to the young people. Private parties would multiply, and the season would close with the Jockey Club ball ; and now, all courtships being brought to a conclusion, and frost having opened the doors of the prison-house, the village would pour out its inhabitants and become, during the winter months, like a city of the dead.

Nothing can be imagined more simple or more fascinating than those Pineville balls. Bear in mind, reader, that we are discussing old Pineville as it existed prior to 1836. No love of display governed the preparations ; no vain attempt to outshine a competitor in the world of fashion. Refreshments were provided of the simplest character, such only as the unusual exercise, and sitting beyond the usual hours of repose, would fairly warrant. Nothing to tempt a pampered appetite. Cards were usually provided to keep the elderly gentlemen quiet, and the music was only that which the gentlemen's servants could produce. The company assembled early. No one ever thought of waiting until bedtime to dress for the ball ; a country-dance always commenced the entertainment. The lady who stood at the head of the dancers was entitled to call for the figure, and the old airs, *Ca Ira, Moneymusk, Haste to the Wedding*, and *La Belle Catharine* were popular and familiar in Pineville long after they had been forgotten, as dances, everywhere else. Ah, well do we remember with what an exulting step would the young man, who had secured the girl of his choice, exhibit his powers of the poetry of motion, when his partner called for the sentimental air of La Belle Catharine. How proudly would he perform the *pas seul* on one side of the column, while his partner did the same on the other ; how gracefully would they unite at

the head of the column, to cross hands ; how tri-
umphantly would he lead her down the middle ;
and when the strain was closing, and the leader
commenced with his bow the prolonged rest on the
final note, how full of sentiment, of grace, and of
courtesy was the bow with which he would salute
his fair lady ! But those are scenes to be lived over
in thought. No untutored imagination can conceive them. They are gone forever. Even in
Pineville they have become things which were.
Time can never restore them ; but so long as an
old Pineville heart beats, so long will be embalmed
in the most fragrant memory, the recollection of a
Pineville country-dance.

The staple dance of the evening was the cotillion.
But as this so much resembles the modern quadrille,
it needs no special description. And now, when a
country-dance, and one or two cotillions, had gently
stirred up the spirits of the dancers, the signal would
be given for the exhilarating reel. A six-handed
reel ! Come back for an instant, thou inexorable
past, and bring again before me that most fascinating of movements ! No lover now claims the
hand of his beloved ; this is no scene for sentiment,
for soft whisper, for the gentle pressure of the
thrilling hand. No ; this is a dance. Your partner
must be a lively, merry, laughter-loving girl ; brisk,
active, animated. Let none venture on it but the
genuine votaries of Terpsichore. There is no room

for affected display. You must retain your self-possession, for the movement is brisk ; but with self-possession there is no fear of awkwardness. The reel is called ; the sets are formed, three couple in each, who generally agree to dance together. The music commences, and off they bound. In rapid succession, we have the chase, the hey, the figure of eight, right and left, cross hands, down the middle, grand round, cross again, and off the whole party darts again, to recommence the intoxicating reel. Has your glove come off ? then dance ungloved, for you have no time to put it on again ; the hands must move as briskly as the feet. And as your pace quickens with intense delight, hark how the fiddlers sympathize with your joy ! Their stamps become quicker, the music plays with accelerated time, and bows and fingers move with a rapidity which Paganini might envy but could never hope to emulate. The powers of endurance are taxed to the uttermost, and set after set retire exhausted. The last set left generally contains some unlucky wight of middle age, who ventures once more to enjoy the luxury of the dance. Now, how wickedly do his young companions (his partner, the instigator) persevere ! How gayly do they strive, by keeping him on his feet, to punish his presumption in venturing among them. But they know not that men of a certain age possess powers of endurance beyond their tender years, and after a pro-

tracted contest find that they have caught a tartar.
The company look on, all parties deeply sympathiz-
ing, and the young are, at last, obliged to acknowl-
edge themselves vanquished.

The reel is the offspring of the genuine love of
dancing. There are none of the auxiliary motives
to learn its movements. No room for the gratifica-
tion of vanity in the display of graceful motion ; no
prurient fancy to be gratified by the privilege of
encircling the waist of a handsome girl, and feeling
her tresses kiss your cheek at every step she takes
in the whirl of the voluptuous waltz, or in the lasciv-
ious movements of the Schottisch, which we once
heard a friend blunderingly, but happily, call a
Sottise. It is a scene of perpetual motion and good
humor. No solemn face may venture on it ; for
laughter, gay and unconcerned, is its proper accom-
paniment. No soft nothings can here be whispered,
for the duties of the dance require your constant
attention ; no graceful insouciance can be tolerated,
for the comfort and happiness of others depend absolutely upon your own good behavior, no less
than upon theirs. Many persons, thinking it too
fatiguing, have fancied that the Virginia reel might
be a happy substitute for it. But this is long and
languid. It is like diluted spirits substituted for pure
champagne. It languished, and, in the phrase of an
indictment, languishingly did live, until, at last, it
died of its own stupidity.

The evening's entertainment was always concluded with the bòulanger, a dance whose quiet
movement seemed to come in appropriately, in order
to permit the revellers to cool off, before exposure
to the night air.   It was a matter of no small importance to secure a proper partner for this dance,
because, by an old custom, whoever last danced with
a lady, had a prescriptive right to see her home.
And this reminds us of another peculiarity of Pineville life, viz., that though every family kept a carriage, nobody ever thought of returning from a ball
by any other mode but on foot.   No carriage was
ever seen in the streets after dark.   The servant,
with the lantern, marshalled the way ; and the lady,
escorted by her partner, was conducted to her home.
And as the season drew towards a close, how interesting became these walks ! how many words of love
were spoken ! how many hearts saddened by the discovery of the hopelessness of an attachment ! how
many persons, now living, whose destinies depended
upon these walks !   To many a dancer the bòulanger was a season of consciousness, of apprehension,
of delight reined in, of hope and of fear ; and there
are numbers still living, in whose recollections a
certain dance of this description will remain in-
delibly fixed.

Besides regular and occasional dancing parties,
riding parties would be got up to promote intercourse between the sexes ; for you must know,

gentle reader, that love became an epidemic in Pineville, just like the fever, and that its exacerbations were always greatest when the season was drawing to a close. The proprietor of a plantation in the neighborhood would invite the young people to drive there on some afternoon and partake of the luxuries of plantation life. Then every young man hastened to secure a partner for the drive; and at the appointed hour, each in his gig (for in in those days gigs were, and buggies were not), the happy party would set off, bound on enjoyment. The amusements on such occasions would be such as spontaneously suggested themselves, but all was apt to terminate in the dance. And sometimes it would happen, that the eager lover, grasping at his opportunity, would pop the question on the outward drive, and if refused, the luckless wight would have to endure the mortification of the homeward drive —*tête-à-tête* with her who had rejected the offer of his love. Oh, blessed be the healing hand of time, which can make the recollection of even such scenes a source of enjoyment !

The serenade is one of the most obvious modes of paying delicate attentions to a lady ; and those who possessed musical skill frequently had their talents put in requisition by young lovers. We almost always remarked, however, the observance of a sort of rigid impartiality in the performance of this attention. If a serenading party went out, every young lady came in for her share of the compliment ; the only distinction being observed was, that the best airs and the longest time were devoted to those for whose favor the entertainment was specially provided.

The season was always closed by the races and the Jockey Club ball. The St. Stephen's race-course, about half a mile from Pineville, is one of the oldest and best in the State. The track runs over a level surface, and within it is a large pond, which, being drained and kept clear of trees, affords from every point an undisturbed view of the horses throughout the race. After the settlement of Pineville, the races were established for the end of October ; and as the season is then comparatively safe, lovers of sport would there meet from various parts of the country. The races, which at that time continued two days, were ushered in by a dinner and concluded by a ball. About fifty years ago, dancers of both sexes drew lots for both places and partners, so that there was, for the first two sets at least, no liberty of choice ; but the practice was discontinued too early for us to have any knowledge of it but from tradition. The purses were altogether made up by a moderate subscription, as no money was taken at the gates ; and though the subscription was general, the stakes were too moderate to tempt the cupidity of professional sportsmen ; so that, I believe, no horse of distinction ever appeared on the course between the years 1794 and 1836. Since that time, the club has been remodelled, the time of meeting changed to January, the subscription increased, and the club now ranks among the most respectable in the State.

Before we quit the subject of amusements in Pineville, it is meet that we conclude by showing one of their most natural issues. Let us take you, reader, to a wedding. The spirit of improvement has pervaded every portion of the State, and a country wedding differs now very little from one celebrated in the city. A Charleston pastry-cook provides the entertainment, and Brissenden's band the music. The company is invited to assemble at a late hour, and no one is expected to stay over to breakfast. But it was not so in days of yore. It was not so when we hailed as a resident of Craven County. The events of 1836 have entirely changed the aspect of society, and the difference between the period before and that since that epoch is as great as is generally perceived in the course of a century. Before the wedding, a visit to Charleston was indispensably necessary. The bride-elect could not think of getting married, without making in person the arrangement of her trousseau. Then, a visit to Charleston was, by no means, an every-day occurrence. An annual visit was common; but there were many who let years pass over without seeing the metropolis. The preparatory visit being made, and all arrangements completed, the day would be fixed and invitations extended. Several days before the wedding the bridesmaids would assemble at the house of the betrothed, and to them were committed all the preparations for the feast. The master of the house furnished the materials, and the busy and active fingers of the bridesmaids transformed them into cakes and confections, jellies, custards, tarts, and all other dainties which the occasion demanded. The master and mistress appeared, as it were, to retire from the management of the household, and leave every thing to the control of those young friends who came to attend their companion to the sacrifice, and to prepare her for it. On the evening appointed the bridegroom (who has been denied the *entrée* to the house since the arrival of the bridesmaids) arrives, the invited guests follow, and, at the hour appointed, the happy couple stand before the priest and receive the nuptial benediction. And, as soon as this is pronounced, the fiddles, which are in waiting, strike up the time-honored air of " A Health to the Bride." Friends and relatives crowd up to offer their congratulations and good wishes, and the poor bride is at last permitted to take her seat, sadly in doubt whether the ceremony itself or the congratulations upon it were the severer trial. Now the waiters appear with tea and coffee, followed up directly with wine, cake, and cordials, and this over, the dancing commences.

The first groomsman opens the dance with the bride, the groom with the first bridesmaid, and, by a time-honored custom, the air is " Haste to the Wedding." After this the dancing continues until near midnight, when supper is announced, and the bride is led into supper by the first groomsman. The supper table is a bona-fide supper table, arranged to hold all the guests. Considerable ingenuity is shown in devising a suitable form, so as to afford the greatest accommodation, and in decorating it. Towers of cake, wreaths, ornaments of every description, may be seen, while by their side an ample provision of turkeys, of ducks, of hams, of rice, and of bread, all showing that it is not a sham, nor designed to be treated as such ; wine, too, flows in abundance ; in fact, the only article which appears to be scarce is water. Toasts are drunk ; jokes fly about, and all are happy, except the parties most concerned, who feel that, though happy, it is too newly to be quite at rest.

After supper the bride disappears. She is no longer seen in the festive hall ; but the music is playing, and the dancing is proceeding, and one by one the bridesmaids drop in, looking very mysteriously, and the dancing proceeds, not the less boisterous from being after supper, and by degrees the elderly folks drop off, and the groom becomes missing, and the hours wear on apace, and the dance becomes more languid, and by two or three o'clock in the morning all becomes quiet, and the parties have sought their beds to recover strength for the duties of the following day.

And herein was exhibited the old-fashioned hospitality of the planters. Every guest was lodged for the night. Beds were arranged everywhere. If the house was too small some out-building was arranged for the occasion. And, O reader, if you were one of the. young men, you would have enjoyed that night, but if you had passed the first excitement of young blood, and were entertaining any vague conceptions of the blessing of repose after a night of revelry, you were doomed to a cruel disappointment. Every device that ingenious youth can invent is brought to disturb your repose. Perhaps on entering your sleeping apartment you find your bed suspended near the ceiling. If you succeed in depositing your wearied body, you are roused by the entrance of a gang of roistering visitors, who come to inquire after your repose. Well! we have had our share of the sport, and must not repine if we have had to witness the day, or rather the night, of retribution. In time, however, even the most restless spirits are exhausted, and by the dawn of day sleep comes to give repose to your wearied brow.

If your lot gives you a bed in the house, your ears are saluted soon after dawn by the fiddlers playing at the door of the nuptial chamber the old air of " Health to the Bride," and somehow it happens that the groom is always the first stirring after this.

As the morning advances the company gradually assemble in the drawing-room, and breakfast is announced. Each bridesmaid presides at a certain portion of the breakfast-table, and the scene here is almost as hilarious as that of last evening's supper. After breakfast the house becomes quiet. The gentlemen mount their horses and ride off, sometimes to hunt—at all events, to take hearty and vigorous exercise, for nothing is more conducive to dispel the effects of last night's dissipation. At two o'clock the company re-assemble ; and on this occasion you will find all the neighbors within visiting distance (which may be twenty-five miles), who are invited to partake of the festivities of the occasion. From the dinner-table the party adjourn to the ball-room, and last night's scene is repeated. On the morning of the third day the party disperses, and the young couple is left to the enjoyment of domestic bliss.

We have already said that the citizens of Pineville were all planters. Unpretending and unambitious, they never sought distinction in the walks of public life. We hope it may not be thought invidious if we notice, among the dead, a few of those who may be considered among the notabilities of the place.

We have had occasion already to introduce the

name of Capt. John Palmer, the father and founder
of the village. By the maternal line he was the
great-grandson of Philip Gendron, the Huguenot
emigrant, who has been more than once named in
this essay. His father, Mr. John Palmer, of Gravel
Hill, was so distinguised for enterprise and success
in the making of turpentine, that he is known by
tradition, even now, after the lapse of more than
seventy years, as Turpentine John Palmer. Capt.
Palmer was an active partisan during the war of the
revolution, and secured the esteem of Marion, who
made him one of his aids. He was a fine model of
a patriarch. Benevolent, his hand was as open as
day to melting charity, but no autocrat could be
more arbitrary. No one dared dispute with him,
for his arguments were all *ad hominem ;* but, by
appearing to yield, the weakest would gain their
point with him. He had never been indoctrinated
in the arts of logic or rhetoric, but his letters, many
of which we have seen, are excellent specimens of
clear good sense and pure idiomatic English. It is
remarkable that this quality of style is by no means
as common now as then, when the means of education were not so easily procurable. After struggling
manfully and successfully through the gloomy and
disastrous period from the commencement of the war
to the introduction of cotton, he died in 1817, aged
sixty-eight years, leaving a large number of descendants by four children, three of whom survived him.

Capt. Peter Gaillard was another of the founders of the village. He was several years the junior of Capt. Palmer, whose eldest daughter he married *en secondes noces*. He possessed an ample patrimony, but in common with other wealthy men, found that, in consequence of the depressed state of the agricultural interest, and the precarious nature of the Santee Swamp, on which his estates lay, his wealth was only a source of expense, and ruin appeared to stare him in the face. The frequency of the freshets in Santee Swamp making it almost impossible to raise corn in it, he purchased, about the year 1794, a tract of land near Nelson's Ferry, in St. John's Berkeley, for the purpose of cultivating provisions. In that year Gen. Moultrie planted cotton on his Northampton estate, in the same parish. The next year Capt. Gaillard tried it on his new purchase, the Rocks, and found that the soil was eminently congenial. His success (Gen. Moultrie's experiment appears to have been a failure) gave an impetus to the new culture, and before the year 1800, cotton was the staple culture of those two parishes. It is about twenty years since Capt. Gaillard's death, and perhaps thirty since he retired from the pursuit of agriculture ; but such was the strength of his mind, the correctness of his observations, and the soundness of his judgment, that it may be doubted whether any material improvement has been effected in the cotton culture since his time.

His opinions are still quoted with respect by those who knew him, and those who never enjoyed that advantage reverently embrace the traditions and ponder over them.   He was a remarkably gentle-manlike-looking man ; one of the last who continued the use of fair-top boots.   He is said to have been fond of carving with his knife, and the balustrades of his piazza bore testimony to this trait.   Having built a fine new house on the Rocks plantation, he abandoned the habit, so far as the house was con-cerned ; but a servant always brought him a cypress shingle after dinner, on which he would indulge in his favorite pursuit.   He was three times married. His first wife, the only one by whom he had issue, was Miss Porcher, sister of the late Major Samuel Porcher.   The second was Anna Stevens, *née* Palmer, widow of Oneal Gough Stevens ; and his third, Caroline Theus, *née* Theus, widow of Mr. Theus, formerly an eminent merchant of Charles-ton.   He left a large family of sons and daughters, and his descendants are very numerous.

Science and humanity mourned, in 1817, the un-timely death of Dr. James Macbride.   He was a native of Sumter district, and was educated at Yale College, where he was a contemporary of Mr. Cal-houn, and of our late venerable bishop.   He en-gaged in the pursuit of medicine, and, settling in Pineville, married Miss Eleanor Gourdin, daughter of the Hon. Theodore Gourdin of that village.   As a physician he was eminently successful, and he was distinguished for sound judgment and a thorough knowledge of his profession. He removed to Charleston to enter upon a wider field of practice, but before he had time to reap any of the promised fruit, fell a victim to yellow fever. The opinions of Dr. Macbride are treasured, and to this day quoted with respect. He had an intuitive perception of truth ; in matters which were the subjects merely of conjecture, subsequent researches have proved the accuracy of his judgments. His recreation was botany. He was the friend and correspondent of Elliott, and assisted largely in the preparation of the botany of South Carolina and Georgia. Mr. Elliott acknowledged the obligation, and in the preface to his work has paid a touching and affectionate tribute to the memory of one who richly deserves his regard and could fully appreciate his own genius. Dr. Macbride left a son and two daughters. His widow survived him many years, and was universally admired for the excellence of her disposition and the elegance of her manners. His son lived but to see manhood. His daughters still survive.

Among the earliest victims of that terrible malady which, for a time, depopulated Pineville, was Dr. John J. Couturier. He was a native of St. Stephen's Parish, was educated at the Pineville Academy, in which afterwards he served as an assistant teacher, and succeeded to the practice of Dr. Macbride. For seventeen years he labored assiduously in his vocation, and his zeal, his activity, his skill, and his unaffected benevolence, secured him the love and respect of a large clientage. His income was large, but hardly exceeded his expenditure, and his friends would often urge him to exact of some of his poor patients a moderate payment—if not in money, at least in articles of country produce, which would be useful to him and convenient for them to spare. But he would never consent. He looked for payment in another world, and would always say that he had a better paymaster than any of his patients could ever be. He died in 1834. His widow, formerly Miss Palmer, daughter of John, and granddaughter of Capt. John Palmer, and their three daughters, still survive.

Mr. Charles Stevens was one of the most respected citizens of Pineville. Feeling himself endowed with talents which he would not willingly permit to lie idle, he was admitted to the bar, and hoped to devote himself to the calling of his profession. But a cruel deafness seized him, which proved incurable, and forever destroyed his hopes. Before it had become so great as to shut him out from social intercourse, he spent two years in the occupation of teacher in the Pineville Academy, and then he engaged in commerce, and opened a store in Pineville, which for many years furnished the

planters with their wants, and brought him wealth.
His deafness increased to such an extent that he
could hear only when the speaker's mouth was applied to his ear. And yet he could always converse
with ease with the members of his family. Mr.
Stevens was an interested observer of politics, and
on all stirring occasions took such an active part, by
means of his pen, that, with his acknowledged
abilities, he was regarded as one of the leading
minds of the late Union party. Thoroughly ex-
cluded, however, from familiar intercourse with
men, he lived very much in a world of his own creation, and his views of politics were better adapted
to a Utopia of his own imagination than to the
actual world. He was universally beloved as well
as esteemed. All his influence was directed to the
cultivation of the literary tastes of his neighbors.
He died in 1833. He married Susan, daughter of
Mr. René Ravenel, and his widow, a son, and three
daughters survived him.

In 1851, Major Samuel Porcher, the last surviv-
ing founder of Pineville, died, in the eighty-third
year of his age. Major Porcher was educated in
England, and on returning home after the war,
commenced his career, as an agriculturist, on his
plantation, Mexico, in St. Stephen's Parish. In
common with all other planters, his life was a struggle until the introduction of the cotton culture,
when he adopted it and cultivated it with great suc-

cess to the end of his life.   He entertained a high
opinion of the value of the lands in Santee Swamp.
He inherited a large estate in it, and made numerous additions by purchase, all of which he determined to secure from the freshets by means of an
embankment.   To this work, therefore, he ad-
dressed himself, and resting his bank on the south
bank of the Santee Canal, he continued it four
miles down the river, where it now stands, the
greatest result of private enterprise, perhaps, in the
southern country.   The embankment is four miles
in length, its base is thirty feet, its height nine feet,
and is so wide at the top that two persons may
very conveniently cross each other on horseback.
By means of this embankment he has reclaimed the
upper portion of the swamp, which now yields large
crops of corn and other grain.   All that is wanting
to render the work thoroughly successful, is a con-
tinuation by his neighbors to the next bluff or
headland on the river.   If this were done, some of
the best lands in America would be redeemed for
cultivation.   The Major was one of the happiest,
the most amiable, and the most popular men in the
State.   At the age of twenty-one he married his
cousin, Harriet Porcher, and they lived together
more than fifty years.   She died in 1843.   Their
home was the abode of elegant and of heartfelt hospitality.   In winter they were rarely without guests,
and at Christmas the house seemed to overflow

with company, consisting not only of their numerous descendants, but of others who, in return for
unaffected kindness, voluntarily offered this grateful
attention. The Major was all his life subject to
asthma, and he smoked incessantly. He eschewed
the Spanish tobacco as a nuisance, but always had
on hand a provision of several thousand American
segars, which were made to his order. He was a
man of great personal activity. and in the last year
of his life managed his horse with the fearlessness
and dexterity of a youth. He had lived so long
with his wife that he could hardly carry back his
thoughts to the time when she was not his companion, and after her death he continued to speak
of her as if she were still alive. He never, like
many others, avoided the mention of her name.
On the contrary, he took a positive pleasure in
making her the subject of conversation. Her say-
ings and doings were spoken of as familiarly and as
naturally as if she still remained at the head of her
family. It ought to be mentioned, as highly credita-
ble to both employer and overseer, that at the time
of his death, his overseer, Mr. Samuel Foxworth,
had lived with him in that capacity upwards of
thirty years. Two sons survive the Major, besides
numerous other descendants by a son and daughter
whom he survived.

Mr. Robert Marion, formerly a member of Congress from the Charleston district, and Mr. Theo-

dore Gourdin, a member from the Northeastern district, both lived in Pineville. Mrs. Anna Peyre Dinnies, now so favorably known in American literature, was also, in her youth, a resident of Pineville, and so was the late Rev. Edward Thomas, rector, formerly of the church on Edisto, afterwards of St. John's Berkeley. John Gaillard, who so many years represented the State in the Senate of the United States, and Judge Gaillard, were both natives of St. Stephen's, but never, I believe, residents of Pineville.[1]

Among the lions of Pineville was John Wall, an Irishman by birth, who lived there in the capacity of factor or general agent for Mr. Theodore Gourdin. He was an old, weather-beaten man, with a

---

[1] Craven County may enumerate, among her notables, the notorious David Hines. This person has been the subject of two biographies, one of which is, we believe, written by himself. We have never read either of them, but the last happening to fall into our hands, during a disengaged hour, we skimmed over a few of the introductory pages, and found them a tissue of falsehoods. He was born in St. Stephen's Parish ; his father was a poor but worthy and inoffensive man ; of his mother we cannot be certain of any information, and choose, therefore, to be silent. He first appeared before the public, as a rider in one of the Pineville races, when, being thrown from his horse, considerable interest was excited in his behalf. He got employment on the plantation of Mr. John Palmer, of Maham's, in the humble capacity of cow-minder, and soon after was charged with the commission of a forgery, the trial for which resulted in his acquittal, but led the way to a subsequent extensive acquaintance with the Court of Sessions. He has no pretensions whatever to the title of M.D., which he assumes. We have always considered his career as a proof of the extreme gullibility of the American people. He has assumed, with success, the best names in the State, without possessing the manners, the address, or even the external appearance of a gentleman, and he is destitute of all talents requisite for the profession of a rogue, except that of matchless effrontery.

great deal of irascibility, tempered with a large stock of benevolence. His predominating idea was attachment to the interest of his patron. He always wore his hair in a *queue*, and on Sundays would appear at church in knee breeches and silk stockings. His veins, which age had enlarged, would show themselves through his stockings, and the irreverent boys would point to them in ridicule, believing that, in order to give more dignity to his shrunk calves, he had stuffed them with paper. He was useful to the public by discharging the duties of a magistrate, and when Mr. Gourdin's influence promoted Pineville to the rank of a post town, Mr. Wall was appointed the postmaster. He had the reputation of being a miser, but we believe he hoarded only for his patron. Mr. Gourdin was a man full of many schemes, which were not very profitable, and Mr. Wall was said to have been never so happy as when his patron was prevented from intermeddling in his own business by his avocations in Washington as a member of Congress. The mutual attachment of the benevolent patron and the humble factor reflected the brightest credit upon each. Mr. Gourdin bequeathed to him an annuity as a token of his sense of the value of his services, but the devoted friend did not enjoy his munificence. He survived his patron but a few months, and appeared to die of a broken heart, lamenting the only man he ever loved.

Before we bring this long and desultory sketch to a close, the nature of the subject appears to call for some remarks respecting health and disease. It was the search after health which led to the settlement of Pineville, and it was the prevalence, long continued, of a fearful malady, which, in 1836, drove the inhabitants to seek refuge elsewhere.

Whoever will consult Mouzon's map of St. Stephen's district, and compare it with the aspect which a map of the same region, if now constructed, would present, will naturally inquire, to what causes such a melancholy contrast is to be attributed. In the palmy days of this parish, the fourteen miles of road, which we described at the commencement of this sketch as leading from the canal to the church, passed in sight of upwards of twenty plantations. And such is the depth of the swamp, and so great was the demand for its valuable lands, that many more were to be found in the interior which were not seen from the road. The first cause of this desolation is to be found in the frequency and the irregularity of the freshets in the Santee River, which have reduced the garden of the State to an absolute wilderness. A few of the names on Mouzon's map are extinct; but the greater part may still be found in St. John's Berkeley, between Monck's Corner and the Eutaw Springs. Before the introduction of the cotton culture, the lands of this last parish were held in very little esteem. Mr. Philip

Porcher had four sons, to whom he left plantations, and he was accustomed to lament the lot of him who had only a place in St. John's. That was the only son who was not compelled to quit his patrimony. The three others, who were left to the inheritance of Santee lands, were all obliged to abandon them, and seek in St. John's the means of making cotton.

How far the unhealthiness of the country may have contributed to its depopulation, it is difficult to say. Our own opinion is, that the insalubrity of our climate has been greatly exaggerated. Nothing is more certain, than that we readily accommodate ourselves to a given standard of health, and scarcely desire any improvement on it. The tone of sentiment on this subject, as well as on others, is, in a great measure, derived from the metropolis, and just in proportion as the sanitary condition of Charleston has improved, does that of the surrounding country appear to have deteriorated. We have seen letters written from Somerton plantation, in midsummer, 1725, in which the writer speaks of having retired thither from the insalubrious climate of Charleston. We have heard the late Mr. Daniel Webb say that, when a child, he was carried from Charleston to the neighborhood of Eutaw, for the benefit of his health. And it was a common practice for the late Mrs. Plowden Weston and her sister, Mrs. William Mazyck, to pay an annual

visit every midsummer to the plantation of their
brother, Mr. Philip Porcher—a great inducement
then being a retreat from the summer heat of the
city and the enjoyment of the luxuries of plantation life at that season. This gentleman died on
his plantation, on Santee Swamp, in 1800, at the
advanced age of seventy. At one period of his life
he had lived in Charleston, but for several years he
resided entirely on his plantation; and we have
often heard it said that, though within six miles
of the village, and having built houses there for
several of his children, he never saw Pineville. Mr.
Edward Thomas, who died at the age of ninety, is
said to have spent forty years without once quitting
his plantation. It becomes, therefore, an interesting
inquiry, what was the state of public health—what
advantage was gained by the settlement of Pineville, and at what price?

The bane of this parish, like that of every portion
of America, south and west of the Hudson River,
was, and is, the intermittent fever of the autumnal
months. This, when of frequent occurrence, becomes habitual, is attended with enlargement of the
spleen, a tendency to dropsy, and a general prostra-
tion of the moral and intellectual, as well as of the
physical man. This disorder was, perhaps, not more
malignant in St. Stephen's than elsewhere; but nature had kindly furnished an asylum wherein the
ague-stricken patient might breathe in safety, re-

cover from his malady, and enjoy the blessing of health, both of mind and of body. This asylum is the pine land. Here is enjoyed an exemption from intermittent fevers.

But this exemption is purchased at a price which is often fatal. In proportion to the salubrity of the climate, is the danger attending exposure to one less healthful. And the price of exposure is not merely a simple and teasing intermittent ; but a fever, sharp, severe, dangerous, and frequently fatal. Few kinds of fever can be named more dreaded by the people of Charleston than the fever which is there found under the name of country fever ; and yet we have often heard Dr. Couturier declare that he had never seen a case of it in the whole range of his extensive practice. Equally dreaded and equally fatal is the myrtle fever of Sullivan's Island ; and yet nowhere do we find a higher enjoyment of health than in Charleston and on the island, the seats of these dreaded enemies. These are the price which the people pay for exposure, and a price of the same kind is exacted everywhere else. So, when the people of Pineville would be alarmed by the visitation of a hot and agonizing fever, which threatened, if not speedily arrested, to terminate fatally, the people of the surrounding country would have no ailments of a more alarming character than the ordinary intermittent of the climate. Now, so highly do we value the sensation of perfect health, that in order to enjoy it we would run the risk of incurring even a worse penalty than country fever. But any violation of the condition of its enjoyment—that is, any exposure at improper seasons, and under unfavorable circumstances—renders one liable to be called upon to endure the penalty. It must be confessed, however, that even when no violation had been offered to the conditions, not only Pineville, but every other pine land, has presented sporadic cases of fevers. There are persons so sensitively and ridiculously alive to the reputation of a place for health, that no case of fever can occur without the cause being diligently investigated ; and this ascertained, how frivolous soever it may be, the poor patient is allowed to die as soon as he may. And it is astonishing how frivolous are the causes which are sometimes gravely assigned and believed. Thus, we remember when the first case of yellow fever made its appearance in Charleston, in 1839, it was said that the young man, its victim, had neglected to provide himself with a sufficient number of towels in going to the bath, and was consequently obliged to spend some time in damp clothes. It never occurred to these good people, that if such a trivial neglect could produce such fatal consequences, it would argue a deadliness of climate which ought to make every one, who has it in his power, to abandon it at once and forever. And we could not but remember how, when a school-boy, we used to run two miles to Maham's mill-pond, and on Saturday spent the whole morning there in the luxurious bath, and no one ever dreamed of a luxury in the shape of a towel, beyond our ordinary handkerchiefs. The truth is, that diseases, fevers particularly, come from God ; to what end, we know not precisely, but a good one, we may be certain. If there were no fevers provided for us, we would be deprived of one of the means for quitting this world ; and it is worse than useless to speculate upon the causes which, in every case, and we believe we may say, in *any* case, generate this disorder.

A pretty extensive observation has convinced us that we know absolutely nothing of the causes of fever. We have seen overseers living year after year in the rice fields of Cooper River, in the uninterrupted enjoyment of perfect health. *These instances are too common to be marked as exceptions.* We have generally observed that those overseers are least sickly who are required to spend their summers on the plantation. We have known others who preserved their health until they resorted to the pine lands. In such cases, our *rationale* of the cause is this : The overseer must be on the plantation late in the evening and early in the morning. If he lives on the plantation, he has no occasion to rise before his usual hour ; if he retires to a pine land, he must abstract from sleep that portion of time which is occupied in going to and returning from the plantation. Now, the summer nights are very short, and though one may without inconvenience dispense with a half-hour's sleep on any given occasion, yet this trifling amount tells in the aggregate, and the climate has full opportunity to work upon the exhausted body. As a general rule, too, the overseers are generally more healthy, whether living on plantations or in pine lands, than men of the same class living on their own pine-land farms. A more generous diet enables them to resist more effectually the effects of the climate ; and we believe that any planter who keeps a good table and enjoys it in moderation, who will not drink too much wine or other stimulating liquors, and who will not suffer his spirits to be depressed by the ominous croakings of his friends, may pass the summer on his plantation, if not in perfect health, at least with no visitation more fearful than the intermittent fever of the climate. The late Dr. Charles Rutledge spent the summer of 1800 on Accabee plantation, and his family enjoyed perfect health. In 1839, when the yellow fever raged in Charleston, and the citadel was full of pestilence, Major Parker removed his family, in midsummer, to the Martello Towers, and they all enjoyed perfect health there. Other cases may without much trouble be enumerated, all going to prove, not that the climate has changed, as our people so rashly

assert, but that the city has become more healthful,
and that our people have a greater fear of fever than
formerly. The great danger to be apprehended is
not the remittent fever, which proceeds by rapid
stages to a fatal crisis, but the slow and lingering
intermittent. As we have before said, it is the repetition of these attacks which breaks down the man.
They tell fearfully, too, upon children, who have
not the strength to bear up against their ravages.
They get ague cakes, and smiles and laughter no
longer play about their little faces, and they know
nothing of the joys and sports of childhood, and their
melancholy countenances prey upon your spirits as
you behold their listless tawny faces ; and at last
God, in his mercy, takes them to himself, and they
trouble this world no more. It is the child, therefore, who has special cause to bless the benevolence
which provides the pine lands. There they feel the
balmy air as it kisses their cheeks, and it seems the
breath of God, inviting them to be happy, and
laughter and childish glee fill the air with their
hopeful and heart-reviving sounds. And let not
the carping critic point to the tombstones which
cluster about the cemeteries of our country, and
show how many have died in childhood, and in
the prime of manhood, even under the favoring
influence of the pine-land air. Regard not their
death. That is the debt of nature. But look to
their lives. If they were happy in life, there is

little to be regretted in their death. But we must return to Pineville.

Though seasons would occur, in which sickness and death would make their appearance in forms more appalling than usual, yet there was generally this consolation, that the rest of the country was equally the subject of the visitation. Thus, in 1817 and 1819, the village was clad in mourning, but disease and death were making hurrying strides everywhere else. In the meantime all the usual appliances for preserving the public health were adopted. The ponds were drained, the ditches kept open, trees encouraged to grow, yard fires kept up every night, and when the village had entered upon its fortieth year, its inhabitants fondly hoped that it was the abode of as much health as Providence deigns award to man. It was in autumn, 1833, that the first cases of that malady occurred, which drove away the people. A gentleman—we believe it was Mr. John Ravenel—was sick. The season was uncommonly dry, and the swamps exhaled offensive odors; his daily rides led him by one of these, and he was supposed to have been poisoned by its exhalations. But he was not alarmingly ill. His fever appeared to intermit, and men began to inquire whether fever and ague was to be one of the diseases of the village. And those who were not connected with him by any ties of intimacy, almost, perhaps quite, forgot that he was sick, when suddenly a ru-

mor flies through the village that he is dying. And
it was even so. The insidious fever, after amusing
his victim for some days, and lulling his friends
into a fatal sense of security, suddenly seized him
with a rigor so intense that neither the patient's
strength could resist it, nor mortal skill successfully oppose it, and before the hot fit could come
on he was dead. Another case of a similar character occurred, and the people gratefully welcomed
the benignant frost, which stopped the progress of
the fever, and opened the doors of their prison-
house. The next summer, 1834, the fever returned,
and in that and the two succeeding summers it continued its ravages, until the most sanguine became
desponding, and the village was almost totally deserted.

And as no cause could be assigned for the fearful
visitation, so health again mysteriously returned to
its ancient abode. By slow degrees the deserted
houses again received their tenants. Men began to
forget their former terrors, and returned, and Pineville is again the abode of a number of planters.
The prestige of its ancient fame still remains, to
give it a sort of metropolitan character over the
neighboring villages of Pinopolis, Eutawville, New
Hope, and others, which have sprung up, like ancient colonies, cherishing the sacred fires from the
hearth of the maternal state. It justly boasts of
its delicious shades, of its clear, cool, and refreshing

water, but it no longer claims a monopoly of health. And while other villages flourish in its neighborhood, and the communication with Charleston has become more easy, the sense of isolation, which once gave its people a peculiar characteristic, no longer is felt, and they have become cosmopolitan. The old times have gone, never to return, and it is to call back the memory of the first fifteen years of our life, and of the two which followed our accession to manhood, that we have made this humble attempt to depict scenes which, though perhaps faded, can never be forgotten. F. A. P.

NOTES.

NOTE A.

THE FRENCH HUGUENOTS.

" To gratify the lusts of power, princes have often encouraged the emigration of their subjects, in the hope of increasing
their wealth and multiplying their possessions. And individuals, led on by an ambitious desire to improve their personal
fortunes, have abandoned the home of their fathers. But none
of these motives prompted our Protestant ancestors to leave
the delightful hills and valleys of their native France. They
were no instruments in the hands of ambitious princes for the
increase of their wealth and power. They did not seek a home
in America, through mere love of adventure, or the ordinary
inducements of pecuniary gain. Far nobler and higher were
the motives that actuated them. They came in search of an
asylum from the relentless persecution of a Catholic rule and
of a cruel government. They sought a home in which they
might enjoy, unmolested, the sweets of political and religious
liberty. They longed to bear away their altars and their faith to
a land of real freedom—a land allowing free scope to the exercise of conscience in the worship of their Maker.

" The name of Huguenot is synonymous with patient endurance, noble fortitude, and high religious purpose. Let us
then be glad that we, a portion of their descendants, are permitted to meet, under the blessed light of liberty and religious
freedom won by them, to pay some imperfect tribute to memories so justly dear, and to remember their fidelity to posterity
and to God. In reverting to the period when a plain but high-

souled, energetic people were driven, by the persecutions of the
Old World, to take refuge in this uncultivated wild, we trace
the origin of this community ; we tread upon the ashes of the
pioneers of religion, of domestic peace, and of social virtue.
To call up scenes of other times, to revive the memories of
the generous dead, to hold up ancestral virtue to praise and
emulation, are grateful tasks, which seldom fail to achieve last-
ing and beneficial results. We look back to our fathers for
lessons of wisdom and piety. We take pleasure in recalling
their brave deeds and their exalted virtues. We like to frequent their accustomed walks and haunts. With pleasure we
sit around the firesides at which they sat, and worship before
the altars at which they worshipped—and who will quarrel
with this just principle of our nature ? Our Huguenot ancestors came out to this country in the complete armor of grown-
up, civilized men. They had been raised under the auspices of
an old and refined civilization ; their minds and hearts had
undergone the severest discipline of an improved age and of
bitter experience. Up to the edicts of Nantes in 1590, stripes,
persecutions, and outrage were exerted against the unfortunate
Huguenots, and in a few years after this they were systemati-
cally proscribed. In the year 1669 an edict against emigration was issued. The Huguenots' worship was openly attacked. No seats in their temples were allowed. They were
prohibited from acting in any branch of the learned profes-
sions. They were not even allowed to pursue the calling of
any business, by which to support their families.

"It was after they were driven from their homes to take shel-
ter in the deserts and forests ; when their property was confiscated, their marriages annulled, and their children declared
illegimate ; when their religious worship was wholly interdicted,
their ministers expelled the country, or if found inhumanly
put to death ; when, in short, all classes of men, women, and
children were hunted down like wild beasts and brutally
murdered while engaged in their religious rites ; it was then,

in these dread hours of trial and suffering, that our fathers conceived the idea of quitting their native land. Had they been rebellious subjects, harassing their sovereign by a vexatious resistance to the laws of the country, or by an attempt to subvert the peace and order of society ; had they been a sect of persecuting religionists, seeking to repress religious freedom or interfering with the dictates of conscience, some apology might be offered for the relentless spirit with which they were persecuted ; but history ascribes to these humble followers of the cross a character wholly different. Quiet and unobtrusive in their manners, devout in their religious exercises, faithful to their king, and obedient to the civil and political laws of their country, they begged only for that peace of conscience attendant on freedom of religious worship, and long bore, with the gentleness of the lamb, the bitter persecutions of their spiritual foes. No violence, no contempt of their rights, no harsh vituperation, could drive them from fealty to their sovereign. From that sovereign they received a dreaded and armed persecution. To him they yielded their hearty obedience in all things pertaining to the legitimate duties of his station. In the successes of their king they seldom failed to rejoice. Over his losses they always lamented, when these involved the honor and glory of France. He received from them sincere condolence for his misfortunes and fervent prayers for his happiness. But the heart of royalty, tempered by a corrupt and crafty priesthood, was steeled against all the blandishments of the pious Huguenots and their cup of bitterness was now full. The fiat of injured nature was gone forth. They resolved no longer to endure the oppressions of a home they loved still so fondly—but as a child loves his parent, who has mercilessly cast him upon the broad bosom of the world friendless and penniless. The impulses of nature were now obliged to yield, to the stern law of necessity ; and they began seriously to prepare to bid adieu to all they loved in their dear native France. " We behold in imagination the vessel as it begins to spread

its sail to the breeze on the distant voyage. We see the devoted group—the grave husband, the anxious mother, the un-
conscious babe—as they crowd the deck to gaze for the last
time upon the receding shore. The bright sun gilds the distant coast, with the rich and varied colors of a summer's land-
scape. Behind those vine-clad hills they yet behold the dear-
est objects of their affections—beloved friends, and the soil that
gave them birth ; all the associations of early life—the remembrance of childhood's home, their native woods and fountains,
their school-boy and school-girl days, and the joy of manhood.
But soon we may imagine them turning their visions to the
blue heavens above them, now spanned by the arch of hope,
and with unwavering courage nerving their hearts to follow on
in the appointments of their heavenly leader. The sufferings
of the mind are worse than those of the body, yet this did our
ancestors brave for freedom of conscience ; nay, more perils
by sea and land and the sickening horror of hope deferred, the
pangs of disappointment and the untold miseries of coloniza-
tion. We cast our eyes towards them in their new homes ; we
see the interesting group. There still are the resolute husband, the brave-hearted matron, and the trembling infant
sheltered in its mother's arm. Casting their eyes through the
forests, they behold with wonder the majestic oak. Excited
by the sublime exhibitions of nature's works, we may imagine
them falling upon the earth and in tears of gratitude sending
up the first evangelical prayer ever offered in these wilds.
From among the thousands who at this time fled from these
violent persecutions, South Carolina received a numerous and
noble population, constituting some of the best families of the
low country—the Marions, Horries, Legares, Desaussures,
Manigaults, Laurens, Hugers, Porchers, Lessesnes, Prioleaus,
Gaillards, Mazycks, Ravenels, Duboses, Couturiers, St. Juliens, and other well-known names ; a race of men gifted
with every manly virtue, who have breathed a high-souled
chivalric spirit into Carolina character, and have added to her

fame. May their memories be ever blessed for their fortitude, and the wise resolve to bear it unstained to a land of spiritual freedom ; and may no blight arise in future to retard our onward progress, or to damp the moral energies of our people ; may generations yet unborn, in dwelling upon the virtues of those who have gone before them, find something to respect and admire in the recollection of our times and our names. May we succeed in acquiring for ourselves a character distinguished for moral and mental beauty, so that in ages to come, when collected multitudes shall be gathered together under these shades to commemorate the virtues of our fathers, there shall be no dark shade in the fair face of our being, to break the bright moral view of the past."

I throw myself on the indulgence of Mr. M. C. Maragne, from whose address, delivered in Abbeville last year, I have selected the foregoing extract.

NOTE B.

MARION'S MEN.

"No monument has been reared to the memories of these men of the swamps, who had fought their country's bravest and most trying battles. They were the men who, regardless of cold, hunger, privations, and fatigue, grappled with the enemy, sprang upon him from the swamp and ravine, surprised and broke up his camps, and drove him from the fields to the city, from the city to the sea. They were the men who, in their own rude way, had hampered, checked, annoyed, and routed the cruel, imperious, and self-sufficient foe. They were the men who, when the regular continental troops had withdrawn from the province, carried on alone the war with the enemy, drove him from point to point, encouraged the troops to return, and in the darkest hours of the struggle restored by their gallant deeds the hopes of the people. They were the men whom sternest suffering could not crush, whom fiercest dangers could not daunt, whom neither hunger, nakedness, cold, privations, nor the gloom of reverses could intimidate or appall. These were the men who, forgetful of their own trials remembered only the afflictions of their country."

The author of the above extract will excuse the liberty I have taken in quoting and adopting his sentiments. I regret that I am unable to furnish his name.